D0105224

Matylda, Bright & Tender

Matylda, Bright & Tender

HOLLY M. McGHEE

CANDLEWICK PRESS

First edition 2017

Library of Congress Catalog Card Number pending
ISBN 978-0-7636-8951-3

16 17 18 19 20 21 BVG 10 9 8 7 6 5 4 3 2 1

Printed in Berryville, VA, U.S.A.

This book was typeset in ITC Veljovic.

Candlewick Press
99 Dover Street
Somerville, Massachusetts 02144

visit us at www.candlewick.com

For McGhee Louise Steiner,
who insisted

"I let time go lightly when I'm here with you . . ."
—Harry Chapin, "Let Time Go Lightly"

*"Daughter, believe me, when you tire on the long
thrash to your island, lie up, and survive."*
—Philip Booth, "First Lesson"

*"Love bears all things, believes all things,
hopes all things, endures all things."*
—1 Corinthians 13:7

Chapter One

If my life were one big calendar and I had to mark my favorite day, I'd put all the shiny gold push-pins I could find on an October morning three years ago. I was standing on the corner with my friend Guy Hose and everyone else, waiting for the school bus. We were six years old. It was cold, the air chillier than usual for a fall day. I was rubbing my arms to stay warm.

"Where's your jacket?" Guy asked. I told him that I left it at home but I was fine. We were going to school, a short trip, not a big deal. But he took off, not worrying about the bus coming, not worrying about what would happen if he missed it. I watched him go, plaid flannel pants running through three backyards—a knight, fearless, jumping over hoses and fences and anything else, no stopping him. He ran right into my house, knowing my jacket hung on a hook in the laundry room. Then he was back, out of breath, with cold-air cheeks, just as the bus pulled up.

I don't think I would have done that. Don't think I would have risked missing the bus to get a jacket for a friend. But Guy, he wasn't worried—all that mattered was me that morning. That's when I knew I loved him—not in a fairy-tale way with a princess and prince or anything like that. I just loved him, the way you love the people closest to you.

Chapter Two

The moment I met Guy is stuck in my mind like rubber cement. I was in kindergarten, and each day at 2 p.m., Mrs. Wolf said, "It's time for free play!" As soon as she said it, almost everybody rushed to the costume corner. It was so crowded and noisy there, with jumpsuits and dresses and costumes going on and off, zippers going up and down, hangers falling off the rack, masks and ties and jewelry all over the place. There were even tap shoes and goggles. It was too busy for me.

I liked the Potato Heads, and they were in a different corner of the room. There were boxes and boxes of them, every size and part you could imagine. It was quiet there, and I had my own Potato Head family. I dressed them the same each day: Mama got the green sneakers and the purple hat, Papa got the yellow shoes and mustache, and Baby Tater only got a bow tie, 'cause he couldn't walk yet. I usually played family with them.

But when Guy arrived, everything changed. Mrs. Wolf introduced him to the class and explained to him that he could do whatever he wanted for free play. He had on baseball pants and a red shirt, and I watched as he scanned the room, seeing everybody in the costume corner and me there, alone with the Taters. Next thing I knew, he was by my side, sitting down with Mama and Papa and Baby and me.

Guy wasn't shy. "Would you like to see a trick?" he asked.

"Sure," I said.

"Okay." He started digging through the boxes of potato pieces, choosing the ones he wanted—quite a few potatoes and lots and lots of ears, some other stuff too.

"Why are you taking all the ears?" I said, wondering if he knew how to play.

"You'll see!" he said.

He took an ear and stuck it through the earhole of a big potato head the opposite way, so the ear was on the inside and the peg was on the outside. He did it again on the other side. The potato looked funny, with pegs sticking out both sides of its head.

"What are you doing?" I said. He didn't answer; he just stuck a new potato on each peg so there were three lined up all together.

"Awesome," I said. Guy added more, and then there were six potatoes in a row. He held it up.

"You know what?" I said.

"What?"

"We could put a potato where the hat is supposed to go! And the feet!"

"Let's do it," he said.

We put more ears inside each potato so the pegs were sticking out the top and bottom, too. Then we stuck on more potatoes.

"It's a never-ending potato!" Guy said. We were both laughing.

"What kind of eyes should we use?"

"Creepy ones," said Guy. I took some eyes out of the boxes.

"Let's use the kind with all the veins," I said.

"Yeah!" And we added eyes to each of the potatoes, six across and four high. We gave them feet too, all different shoes and sneakers, so the never-ending potato could stand on whichever side it felt like.

From then on, I shared my corner with Guy—we could hardly wait till 2 p.m. each day. We couldn't wait to build another never-ending potato.

Chapter Three

We had a school-wide picnic at the end of first grade. I'd known Guy almost two years already, and we were good friends, but not together-all-the-time friends. My dad volunteered to bring ice pops, 125 cherry ice pops, and he showed up when a bunch of us were playing kickball. I saw him coming from the car—I couldn't mistake my dad, tall and thin, with a Hawaiian shirt, khaki shorts, and a giant mound of hair.

"Ice pops!" my dad yelled, and everybody started running. "Line up, ladies and gentlemen—one pop each!" But Guy didn't come. He was kneeling, out in right field.

"Guy," I said, running back toward him, not wanting him to miss the pops. "My dad has ice pops!"

He didn't get up. "Guy," I said, getting closer. "My dad—"

"Look," he whispered, turning toward me. "Look what I have." There was a ladybug on his fingertip, with delicate black dots speckled on a coat of red, her teeny wings fluttering as she walked around his finger. I knelt down beside him and put my finger next to his. The ladybug took flight and landed on my hand. I held my breath as she explored.

"Do you believe she brings good luck?" I said softly.

"I don't just believe it," whispered Guy. "I know it."

"How?" I said.

"Because of my dad," said Guy. "He was out in the garage a few years ago, trying to make kindling for our woodstove. The wood he used was damp, and he was holding it in place with one hand while bringing the ax down to sliver it off with the other. Me and my mom were in the living room when we heard him yell, 'ALBERTA, WE'RE GOING TO THE EMERGENCY ROOM.'

"We'd never heard his voice like that, and he usually called her Bertie; we knew it was serious. His thumb was nearly severed from his hand, and Mom wrapped it in rags and T-shirts and towels to stop the bleeding. We got him in the car, and she reclined his seat all the way back, and then she rested his arm, wound up in all that cloth, on the open window. 'Just keep it higher than your heart if you can, Jacques,' she said, making sure it would stay. 'That'll stop the bleeding.'

"She turned to come back to the driver's side, but Dad stopped her. 'Bertie,' he said, 'It'll be okay. Look . . .' And he drifted off. Mom and I saw what he was talking about; a ladybug had landed on his wrapped-up hand, right on the end where his thumb was supposed to be.

" 'Did you see that, Guy?' my mom said. 'It'll be all right. A ladybug landing brings luck.'

"My father didn't lose his thumb. They sewed it back on and reconnected most of the nerves; they couldn't get them all, but it works pretty well. The ladybug brought us luck, staying on his hand all the way to the hospital, even with the open window."

My dad came over then, a cherry pop in each

hand. "Lucky you," he said. "I have two pops left." Me and Guy looked at each other with big eyes, hardly believing my dad's words.

"Guy," I said, when my dad headed back. "Are you thinking what I'm thinking?"

"The ladybug strikes again!"

"Wow," I said. "I guess they can bring luck for everything—the big things and the little things. Your dad's thumb and our ice pops, too."

"Yeah," said Guy. "I never thought of it that way."

From then on, me and Guy looked out for ladybugs, at recess or whenever we got to eat lunch outside. Sometimes they showed up on a windowsill, a swing set, or even on somebody's hair—we were always on the watch, Sussy and Guy of the Ladybug Landing.

Chapter Four

My dad called us spaghetti and meatballs, 'cause we could usually be found together, and one Friday after school, in the spring of fourth grade, we sat down to have our regular snack: a not-so-little pile of Pringles, the only junk food my mom allowed (she liked the way they stacked), and a glass of ginger ale. She said it was good for your stomach.

Mom was also the reason we were at the dining table in the first place. She was a why-notter, from *why not* believe in God to *why not* eat in the dining room under a beautiful chandelier. She had a good point, and the chandelier was pretty, so we ate our snacks and played Monopoly there too.

Guy and I laid out the board, tucking in our money, lowest to highest. Like always, I put my five-hundred-dollar bill all the way under, saving it for when I really needed it, while Guy left his out, front and center, ready to be spent. "I'll see if my dad wants in," I said.

Dad was in the basement at his laptop, working on his new self-help book, this one about couples who don't compromise. I had a hunch it was inspired by him and my mom, because they both have strong opinions about most everything, including my name. Since they couldn't agree on what to call me when I was born, my dad picked one name and my mom picked another. My first, Susquehanna, came from the Susquehanna Trading Company, based in New York City, where my dad used to work. That's where he built our family's "nest egg"—the money that gave him the cushion to try writing books. "It stands for freedom," he said.

My mom chose my middle name, Indiana, and it wasn't about the prairie state. She was a big fan of Indiana Jones from *Raiders of the Lost Ark* and all the ones after. "For strength," she said.

The funny part is that they both ended up calling me Sussy.

"Gonna play, Dad?" I asked. He rolled back in his chair, running his hand through his hair.

"Hmm," he said. "Should I or shouldn't I?"

"We've got chips," I said. "Sour cream and onion."

"Monopoly and Pringles. A doubleheader. I'm in." He followed me up the stairs.

Guy went with the iron, I took the car, and my dad got the wheelbarrow. "You know what Guy's mom says, right?" I asked my dad.

"What?"

"Everything you need to know about life can be learned from Monopoly."

"Is that so?"

"Yup, it is, Mr. Reed," said Guy. "At least according to her. Addition, subtraction, buying, selling, and strategizing."

"But what about luck?" my dad said. "Do you learn that?"

"Luck's another story," said Guy. "You just get it, sometimes good, sometimes bad. Unless there's a ladybug, of course—then it's always good." I thought about Guy's bad luck in the last game we'd played. He ran out of money, mortgaged everything, and then landed on my brand-new hotel on Pennsylvania Avenue. End of story. Except that I didn't enjoy winning very much 'cause I had to watch him lose.

As usual, Guy bought everything he could, and I was more strategic, buying properties with the highest rents. We both had monopolies pretty fast, but not my dad, because he only ever bought reds and purples. "Why are you so stuck on those colors?" I asked him.

"Research," he said. "Trying to see if you can win by not compromising." His logic was crazy, but so was he, and we didn't mind. Not surprisingly, he went bankrupt pretty fast, and then all that mattered was the dice. I landed on Guy's properties and he landed on mine, and it seemed like the game could go on forever.

"I'm bored," I said.

"Boredom," my dad replied. "Something else Monopoly teaches you. Gotta hand it to your mom, Guy. Everything you need to know about life can be learned right here." He tapped the board. "Between the two of us, I bet we've got the makings of another book."

I thought about Mrs. Hose and how many times I'd heard her say that about Monopoly. In some ways it was true; I did learn to strategize and count money. I learned that you could pick up a card from the middle of the board and go directly to jail and then just as easily pick up a different card and get out of jail free. And I learned that you could land on a big red hotel on Boardwalk and watch your fortunes change in an instant. It was business and luck, but that wasn't everything.

"I know what's wrong," I finally said. "There's no love in this game."

My dad made a frowny face. "Banana peels," he said. "You're right."

I laughed 'cause that's what Dad said whenever there was something he hadn't thought of, like *boom,* he'd slipped on a banana peel.

"Plenty of other places for love," my dad said. "You've got us and you've got each other. Isn't that enough?"

"Not really," I said. "We don't have siblings or anything."

My dad seemed concerned.

"We need a pet," I said. "That's what's missing.

Are we ever going to get one?" It was something I'd asked for so many times that I'd pretty much given up. But it was worth another try.

"You know what your mom says, right?"

"Yes. 'There's enough animals in the house already,'" I said, quoting her. "Not funny. We're just hoping for something to love that's all our own, Dad."

"I know what I'd choose," said Guy. "I mean, if we could get one."

"Let me guess," said my dad. "A leopard gecko."

"Right," said Guy. He had wanted a leopard gecko since our animal unit at the beginning of third grade, and he had read everything there is to know about them, but Mrs. Hose said they didn't have room for a pet. It was one of the few things she said absolutely no to.

"What about a bird?" I asked.

"Oh, no, you don't," my dad said. "I had one once. First you stare at it in the cage and then, when you let it out, it leaves droppings everywhere, mostly out of reach."

"So you can't clean it up but you know it's there?" I asked.

"You *can* clean it up," he said. "But you need scaffolding to get to it."

"Ew," I said. "Guinea pig?"

"They don't do anything except squeak once in a while," said Guy. "We had one in preschool."

"Wait a sec," said my dad. "Who said you could have a pet?"

"Can we?" I said. "Please?"

"Are you really ready to take care of it?"

"We're not babies."

"I promise," said Guy. "And I vote for the gecko."

"I'm not sure about that," I said.

"Listen," said Guy. "They're good beginner reptiles, and they don't smell. You keep them in a tank; they don't just crawl around the house." Guy was getting going now. "If you want, you can just use paper towels for substrate. That's what you line the bottom of the tank with." Guy ran his hand along the table and looked up at Dad.

He was winning me over. I jumped in. "I think it could be good for us, Dad. We wouldn't have to walk it or anything. We could keep it in my room."

"Your mother would appreciate that."

"Mr. Reed, we'll love it like crazy!" said Guy. "It'll be something all our own."

It felt like the stars lined up for us right then, 'cause my dad seemed to understand, and he ran his hand through his hair again. "That's hard to resist," he said to us both. "I want you to have something of your own, too." He sighed. "It's part of growing up, isn't it?"

And not very long after that, the three of us were in the Honda, backing out of the driveway.

Chapter Five

"How can I help you?" a skinny salesclerk in a Total Pets T-shirt asked when we walked in the door. He looked like a high-schooler, and according to his badge, his name was Mike. "Goldfish?"

"No goldfish for us," my dad said. "We're here for a gecko."

"That's a broad term," Mike said. "So many fantastic species—"

"A leopard gecko," Guy said.

"Clarity," said Mike. "That's what I'm looking for. Follow me, folks." He showed us a twenty-gallon tank with three leopard geckos inside. "The two smaller ones just arrived from the breeder," he said.

"That larger one, with all the dark spots, she's been here awhile—from before I even started. Take a look."

"That's her," Guy said, on his knees, pointing to the larger one. She was near the glass, her face staring into Guy's.

"How do you know?" I said. I was watching the smaller ones, crawling in and out of a log. They were more playful. I crouched down by Guy and looked at the big one. Her eyes were black, and she blinked. Her skin was dark, too, with patches of yellow peeking through. She was locked on Guy.

The little ones were out of sight, hiding in the log, as the big one came even closer, opening her mouth and showing us her tongue. We were both pressed against the glass. And then she nodded, right at Guy, with the whole of her long neck and head. Like she was saying to him, "You there, you with the glasses. Hurry up now and take me home."

"She means business," I said. "I think she told the little ones to get out of the way."

"I wouldn't doubt it," said Guy. "It's like she knew we were coming."

Guy could be so easy to convince sometimes.

One year his mom bought a dozen boxes of Girl Scout cookies, and she put them in the freezer for safekeeping.

"These are special cookies," she told us. "They're equipped with a satellite radar that will signal me if anybody opens a box without permission." I rolled my eyes at Guy when she said that, because I knew that Girl Scout cookies didn't come with satellite detectors. But Guy believed her.

"It can't be true," I told him one afternoon, pulling a box of Thin Mints out of the freezer. Guy tackled me, holding my hands to my sides so I couldn't open the box. He grabbed it and put it back in the freezer.

"Ow," I said. "You could have hurt me. You really believed her, didn't you?" He shut the freezer door. "She doesn't actually have a radar on the cookies, that's not even possible. She's just trying to keep you out of them."

"Don't eat them," Guy said, and I didn't say anything back, 'cause I knew Guy wouldn't risk it and I couldn't convince him.

So I went along with him and the big gecko too, even though I wasn't 100 percent sold on her—just like with the cookies, I knew Guy wouldn't budge when he was convinced. There weren't very many to choose from, either, and Mike said she'd been here awhile. This could be her one chance. "What should we name her?" I said.

"Let's see," said Guy. He studied her, and so did I. Her eyes were shiny, with a slit down the middle from top to bottom. Her face, scaly and dry, seemed as though it had been around for centuries, and her feet had gritty little toes that looked like starfish.

"What if we call her Matylda?" he said. "With a *y* so it's all her own."

"Matylda with a *y*," I said to her, and she turned to me, saying hello, as if she liked the name. "Matylda of the Ancient Face and Starfish Toes."

"Matylda it is," said Guy. "And her toes *are* starfish—you're right."

My dad filled our cart with accessories. He wasn't always easy to win over, but once he came around, he came around all the way and then a little more, and soon we had a fifteen-gallon tank, a heating pad, a reptile carpet, a light, a water pool, two privacy logs, and two plastic palm trees. He got a leopard gecko manual too, not that it was necessary with Guy around.

My dad added another log to the cart. "Just in case she's shy," he said. "She'll be able to go under-cover." I was thinking, *Let's not go overboard, Dad,* but I was happy he was so enthusiastic.

"Once she settles in," Mike said, "feed her crickets. Live crickets. I'm glad you took that one—glad you found your match."

"We've got plenty of crickets in the yard," my dad said. "Be fun to try to catch some. Thanks for your help, son." He signed the exotic-pet permit and we left the store.

Guy was my best friend, and now we had a pet. Matylda was lucky, because I knew Guy would put her first, too—the same way he had with me at the bus stop, when he ran to get my coat.

Chapter Six

Matylda lived in my room—her tank fit right on top of my dresser, which was wide and not too tall, with a large mirror attached. She had a choice. She could see the world as it was, or as a reflection. When Guy looked at her, she looked right back, eyes to eyes, till he finally grinned and broke the hold.

"She definitely knew we were coming," he said, bringing in a stool for me and one for him.

"I really think she got those other two lizards to hide so you would pick her," I said. In the mirror Matylda was watching me. "I think she heard that."

"Yeah, I bet so," said Guy. "Those two things that look like holes in the sides of her head are actually ears. She's got excellent hearing."

"I'll watch what I say then." I leaned in to look at her ears. "I can see right through her head," I said.

"Yup," said Guy. "That's what a solid ear canal looks like."

"Do you remember the Taters?" I said. "How we put their ears inside their heads?"

"Of course," said Guy. "But now we've got to help her adjust to the hand. That's important and it can take a while."

"Okay," I said. "What do I do?"

"Best if she comes to you on her own," he said. "So put your hand in the tank and wait. Don't move it a lot or she might get scared."

I didn't want to go first, didn't want to stick my hand in the tank. It seemed as though she liked Guy better already.

"You go first," I said.

"All right. Come here, Matylda with a y. I've been waiting for you my whole life!" Guy slowly placed his hand on her brown reptile carpet, and Matylda walked right over and climbed on. Then, with no hesitation, she walked up his arm and curled behind his neck. "She's cold-blooded," he said, holding his head steady, "so she likes my body warmth."

I watched her there, nestling in, under his hair. She seemed to feel right at home with Guy. She peered at me from that warm place on his neck.

"She sure likes it back there," I said.

"It feels nice," said Guy. "But I can't sit like this forever. You try it." I thought Matylda understood, because she crawled down from Guy's neck, one step at a time, not scared and not in a hurry. But when she got to the bottom, she stayed on his wrist.

"Touch her," Guy said. I reached out my finger and touched her back. I was nervous—she was exotic and rough and could move quickly.

"Lay your hand out," he said. "And relax." I took a deep breath and laid my hand near her, but she didn't come.

"Don't you like me?" I said, looking straight into her black eyes. She blinked and kept the hold, but she didn't come onto my hand. Maybe she was saying no.

"Not quite ready, Matylda with a *y*?" Guy said. "That's okay—you're doing great." He picked her up around the belly. "You should go back in the vivarium now, anyway," he said.

"Vivarium?"

"That's the tank," said Guy.

He put her in.

Matylda yawned.

"She's had a lot of activity," Guy said. "She's probably tired."

"Take a nap," I said to her. "Go ahead." It would be nice to have Guy to myself for a while.

Matylda yawned again. And then she came right up to the glass and opened her mouth, yawning very widely this time. "Maybe she's hungry already," Guy said. "She does seem to be settled in."

Guy turned to Matylda. "Are you hungry?"

Matylda nodded. "That's a yes," he said. "I guess she's not tired."

"Do we *have* to give her live crickets?" I asked Guy.

"Mike said so, remember? She's got to stalk her prey!"

"It's kind of gross, though."

"But you'll love it, won't you?" he said to Matylda. "We'll be back."

We found my dad in the basement. "Mr. Reed," said Guy, "we have a problem."

My dad looked up.

"Uh, not a problem exactly. We just need crickets for a very hungry lizard."

"We've got a hungry gecko, do we?" my dad said. "Like I told Mike, it'd be fun to try to catch some. There's plenty in the yard. Be a shame to buy them. I'm not fast enough, though."

"Me neither," I said quickly.

"I'm fast," said Guy. "But not quiet."

My dad liked challenges. He was kind of like a Cub Scout that way. "Hmm," he said. "We need a simple one-way trap, with something to lure them in." He got up and looked around his workroom. "Channeling your mother now," he said. "*Why not* soda bottles, with a tasty lure inside?" He took two bottles out of the recycling bin and grabbed some scissors off the pegboard. He cut the bottles in half and tossed out the bottoms.

My dad took the cap off one of the half bottles and nested the capless bottle, headfirst, inside the bottom of the other half bottle, the one with the cap still on. "Voilà!" he said. "Let's get some bait."

We went upstairs, and my dad handed Guy a baby carrot. "Drop in the lure. If my theory's correct, the less intelligent crickets will assume that the carrot comes without a price. Those crickets will enter the bottle, and once they do, they won't be smart enough to turn around and go out the hole they crawled through to get in. That's the trade-off. They get to nibble the carrot, and we take them prisoner!"

Guy dropped the carrot straight through the neck into the trap.

"I get it," said Guy, shaking the carrot around in the bottle. "Once the cricket goes in, it can't really change its mind."

"Right," said my dad. "No going back."

"There's really just one way out," I said. "Into Matylda's tank." It was the worst possible outcome for the cricket, but if Matylda needed to stalk prey, I was going to have to adjust to crickets meeting an untimely end. It was hard to believe that a simple Monopoly game had gotten us here. But at least the crickets were plentiful, if the cheeping I heard at night was any indication. We weren't taking the last of the species or anything.

It was close to six, time for Guy to go home for dinner. It wasn't that he cared about eating on time, but food was a focus for Mrs. Hose. So we set the trap in the rhubarb patch, and Guy yelled to the world, "ENTER IF YOU DARE!" He was talking to the crickets, of course, but only I knew that. He turned to me and said, "Hands off the trap till I return."

"Not a problem," I said. No way was I going to check it alone.

Guy put on his helmet, hopped on his bike, and began to pedal, turning back to wave as he rode down the street. He kept looking back and waving as he pedaled away, not even watching where he was going. It made me think about sledding over the winter.

We loved to go to Flood's Hill, one town over, and Guy got a thin-as-paper flying-saucer for Christmas, the color of aluminum foil, with one fabric handle on each side. I got a big snow tube, a giant puffy doughnut—I think our parents must have planned it. We went right to Flood's Hill the next day. Guy slipped the rope pull from my tube through his flying-saucer handles, and we went down tethered like that, almost getting dumped—a slick fast ride on the icy slope.

Then Guy had the idea of going down together on one sled, so he sat in the back of his saucer, and I sat inside, knees pulled up tight. We hit a big bump, the saucer popped up, and we landed backward, continuing down the hill that way, not able to see where we were going.

On the way up again, Guy said, "Sussy?"

"Yeah?"

"Were you scared?"

"A little."

"When we were backward?"

"Yeah," I said. "I didn't know where we were going."

"Me either," he said. "It was like we were backward and forward at the same time."

"I'm okay with it," I said. "As long as you're with me!"

"Me too," said Guy.

My mom was an event planner, and she often had to stay late in the city. When she finally got home that night, she poked her head into my room to meet Matylda. I wasn't quite asleep yet. "I'm happy for you and Guy," she said. "Happy that you have a new playmate."

"We do," I said. "But she won't come to my hand yet. I think she likes Guy better."

"Just give her time," my mom said, walking over to the tank and tapping on the glass.

"You're lucky to have her," she said to Matylda. "You hear that?"

Matylda didn't acknowledge my mom, but she was awake, crawling around her tank. I hoped she was listening, hoped she agreed.

Chapter Seven

The next morning, the doorbell woke me up, and I got right out of bed 'cause I knew Guy would keep ringing till I let him in. From the top of the stairs, I could see him, his eyes big and eager, his mouth smiling through the panes of glass. "It worked it worked it worked!" he yelled. I threw on my sweatshirt, right over my pajamas, just to get to the door before my parents woke up.

"I sort of hoped we wouldn't catch any," I said.

"Why?" asked Guy.

"I don't feel that good about killing crickets."

"We're not going to kill them," Guy said. "Matylda is. They're just feeders."

I doubted the crickets considered themselves just feeders.

"If we didn't have a lizard, I bet you'd call them crickets," I said.

"But we do have a lizard," he said. "And we have to take care of her. She has to stalk!" I followed Guy out to the rhubarb, and he showed me the crickets, three of them, bouncing around in the bottle like pinballs. They were primitive and sharp, their spiky legs meant for jumping, their eyes beady, antenna long.

"Last night, they were just three comrades play-ing in the rhubarb, figuring they had a lot more nights like that to come," I said. "One of them prob-ably saw the orange color, smelled the carrot, and thought it would be tasty. The others followed to stick with their friend. Anybody would do that, fol-low a friend's path to stay together."

"You've got to think of them as feeders," said Guy, holding the trap in front of me. "Feeders who have each other. Your dad's trap design worked!"

That was true. My dad would be thrilled. As for the crickets, Guy was correct; they were together, even if they'd soon be together in Matylda's stomach.

I had to accept it, 'cause I didn't want to ruin the fun for Guy—he was so excited that the trap had worked, and getting a lizard had been his dream. It almost seemed like he loved her as much as he loved me. We ran to wake my dad.

"Mr. Reed," said Guy. "It worked it worked it worked!"

"That's what all the noise was about," he said. He nudged my mom. "Ivy," he said, "you've got to see this."

The crickets still bounced as my dad pulled back the screen top to the tank. "Hold the trap vertically and unscrew the cap," he instructed Guy. The crickets were at the neck of the bottle with the baby carrot. Guy took off the cap and shook the bottle while my dad tapped a few times—the crickets shot head-first into Matylda's tank.

"Eat and flourish!" Guy said, just like his mom always did.

"Close the screen!" I shouted from up on the bed. I didn't want to find a feeder in my room later.

"All the way!" my mom said from the door-way. That's something I shared with my mom—we weren't bug people, even if they were comrade crickets.

Matylda took in her new company, as if she had done this thousands of times before. Then it was over so fast—a stalk, a snap, an antenna or two sticking out of her mouth, and a gulp. Clean and bloodless. On to the next. I watched her use the mirror, and I was even more sure that she was clever. She eyed her next victim without attracting any attention at all, and then, at once—*whoosh*—she sprang and twisted and attacked. The cricket had no chance. After the third hunt, Matylda looked straight at us, still as a photograph, except for one final antenna sticking out of her mouth, a long one, twitching.

"She's impressive," said my mom. She looked at me, still up on the bed. "You doing okay with your new roommate?" she asked.

"I'll get used to it," I told her. "She's got to stalk her prey. At least she's fast."

"I'll say," my dad agreed. "Nice work, Matylda. We'll catch some more for you tonight. We can probably use apples for bait, too, just in case they get wise to the carrots." He and my mom left the room.

I couldn't stop looking at the antenna sticking

out, still moving back and forth, slowly, the singular reminder of what had just happened. The rest of the cricket was inside Matylda. As if he could read my mind, Guy said, "Sussy?"

"Yeah?"

"You worried about the cricket?"

"Yeah."

"Because of its antenna?" he asked. We were both quiet.

"It's between two worlds," I said. "You know what I mean?"

"Kind of."

"I mean, the antenna is still in this world, but the rest of her isn't anymore . . . like the cricket's here and somewhere else at the same time."

"I get it," said Guy.

"Do you think lizards can feel happiness and sadness, or just heat and cold?"

Matylda was watching me, sizing me up.

"They can feel everything," he said. "Just look at her."

"I think so, too. Do you know where she came from?"

"You mean before she got to Total Pets?"

"Yeah."

"We could ask Mike," he said. "But my house first, for the best waffles on earth."

"Good idea," I said. "Maybe when we get back, that antenna won't be sticking out."

The Hoses were picky about bikes, so we put ours in the garage as soon as we got there. We didn't want to hear "A rusty bike is worse than none at all, and it can rain anytime, even when the sun is out" ever again.

Touch the bell heart/hear it jingle, I said to myself, looking at the ornament on the Hoses' door. Guy's mom had told me more than once the bell heart was a wedding gift—and I loved the Christmas-y sound of the tiny red metal bells.

I remembered a summer dinner we had with the Hoses the year before—deviled eggs and Ramapo tomatoes with fresh basil and mozzarella cheese—a cool breeze blowing through the screened windows. "I surrender to the Ramapo," said Mr. Hose. "The perfect blend of sweet and acid." He speared one with his fork, holding it up for us all to admire. "Nothing like it," he said.

But then he frowned. "A shame I have to go away tomorrow; do you think I can take some in my carry-on?" Mr. Hose wasn't around that much 'cause he traveled for work, but when he was home, he usually made us laugh.

"Do you miss your dad when he's not here?" I asked Guy after that dinner. "Do you wish he were here all the time, like my dad is?"

"That'd be cool," said Guy, "but he doesn't stop being my dad just 'cause he's on a trip."

"I get it," I said.

I touched the heart, and we went inside, and as soon as Mrs. Hose heard us, she said, "Waffles almost ready. How's the lizard-who-doesn't-live-*here*-thank-goodness?"

"You've got to see her hunt," said Guy. "You're not afraid of crickets, are you?"

"That depends," said Mrs. Hose. "In general, or if I find one in the shower?"

"Which would you rather?" said Guy. "Be thrown into a tank of crickets or a tank of lizards?"

"That's a horrible question with an easy answer," said his mom. "Neither."

"One or the other," said Guy.

"Lifeline to Sussy Reed," said Mrs. Hose. "Help me decide."

We played this game a lot. "Well," I said, "depends what you prefer. Crickets have crackly shells and gooey insides and they like to stick with their friends," I said. "Beady eyes, too . . . and they can jump really high." I started putting butter on my waffle.

"Have mercy," said Mrs. Hose. "Not sounding good."

"I'll tell you about lizards, then," said Guy. "They shed their skin and grow new teeth every four months. And they leap!"

"Not good either," she said. Her hands were on the table. "I'll go with my first instinct. Neither."

"Mom," said Guy, "that's not an answer. You know how this game works. Make a decision!"

"That changes the lay of the land," said Mrs. Hose. I'd eaten half my waffle already. "Can lizards climb?"

"Not leopard geckos," Guy said. "No toe pads."

"Lizards, then," she said. "Though I'd hang from

the top so they couldn't touch me. That's got to be better than being trapped with gooey-inside stick-together crickets that jump."

"Did you know that lizards eat crickets in a single gulp?" I asked.

"You're sure?"

"Yup. They kill them with their teeth and then the cricket goes down in one piece," said Guy. "We witnessed it this morning."

"Lordy," she said. "I'm glad we don't eat our protein like that."

We finished our waffles, and before going back to my house, Guy and I walked over to Total Pets so we could ask Mike about Matylda. We found him by the fish. "Hey," said Mike.

"Hi," said Guy. "Remember the gecko we bought yesterday?"

"Of course! What can I do for you?"

"Well, we want to know where she came from, before she got to the store."

"That's a good question I can't answer," he said. "She was bred in captivity—I know that. She's not from the wild."

"That's it?"

"'Fraid so," Mike said. "But you got a special one, with all those dark spots. Never seen one quite like her. Give her a story of your own—she'll love it," he said. "Tell her why you adopted her. Give her an identity."

"Just make it up?" Guy asked.

"Why not?" said Mike, and I grinned, 'cause Mike had a lot in common with my mom.

"Yeah, why not?" I said. "Thanks, Mike."

Chapter Eight

"You want to know your story?" I asked Matylda when we got home. "You want an identity?" Her eyes were curious. Of course she wanted to know her story. She was about to become more than just a common leopard gecko from Total Pets. I laid my hand in the tank, but she didn't climb on.

"She won't come to me," I said. "Why does she come to you and not to me?"

"Maybe she just wants to stay in there," Guy said. But when he put his hand in, she came right over. He placed her on his leg, and she rested on her elbows, starfish feet together in front. It seemed like the two of them were everything to each other then, like they might have forgotten I was even in the room.

"Okay then, let's go," Guy said, grabbing a towel and putting it over his head. "I'm getting in touch with your spirits." He looked silly with the towel, but I kept quiet. I didn't want to be disrespectful of Matylda's origin story. "Your history's filtering through, getting less hazy," Guy said. He moved his hands like he was cleaning glass, not missing any specks of dirt. "Clearing, yes . . . yes, it's here. We're . . .

"High atop a mountain, in Pakistan. You are with your master. Wait—what do I see? He's next for the throne." Guy's voice got lower. "Your master, he is greedy. He wears layers of robes, embroidered with jewels—I'm getting closer now. Wait! Ah, I see. Beneath the clothes, he is puny." Guy focused. "He will be king one day, but for now, time passes slowly. Not much to do in his castle. He relies on you and your fellow lizards for entertainment, forcing you to duel each other till death." Matylda didn't move as she listened to Guy—she was right there on the mountain with the tiny future king.

"Terrible what I see now," said Guy. "Your master, he captures all the lizards he encounters on his daily trek down the mountain and up again, his training for the day he will be king. Ah, here we are now, in the holding cell, dirty, with very little light. I see you, Matylda, in a tank, hungry, thirsty—all part of his plan. He brings his lizards to the point of near starvation, to the point where they will eat each other to live. You're there in the corner, tail curled tight around your head." Guy's voice was a low whisper now.

"You are crying, but the tears are dry from lack of water. A great warrior you are, having beaten your opponents forty-nine times in a row. For each victory, each death, you have been given a black spot to mark the toll you've paid, for you carry the sadness of the forty-nine dead lizards in your heart." Matylda twisted her head and looked back at her spots.

She was covered with them; she closed her eyes and bent her head. I could feel her sorrow, the sorrow of a survivor. She sat in that holding cell for days, maybe months, knowing the only way out was to kill. The weight of every lizard who fell by her own hand would be with her for always. I saw her differently then.

Guy continued: "Your master made a decree, up and down the mountain. On the occasion of winning your fiftieth duel, you'd be granted your freedom and a wish. But remember: Your master took pleasure in the pain of others, and he saw to it that your fiftieth duel was nearly impossible to win. He set you to fight a lizard twice your size.

"Word had spread about you, Matylda, the warrior with heart who'd never been beaten. You were neither large nor especially strong, but your senses were keen, and with your fiftieth duel approaching, it quickly became known that the great warrior lizard was fighting her last. The stakes were high: on the one hand, death; on the other, freedom and a wish.

"The battle commenced," said Guy. "Your opponent was freshly captured, with no spots at all. He had not been subject to the holding cell, not deprived of food and water. The match was as uneven as a match could be. The future king showed little mercy, even on the day of what would surely be, one way or another, your last battle.

"Your opponent, eager, charged you, but you knew his game, for you had fought many before him. You went flat to the ground, and he met the wall at tremendous speed. He weakened. What the future king didn't know was that your opponent was no match for your intelligence. You outwitted him, round after round, flattening, swerving, ducking. The opponent? He died there, against the wall, charging and missing one last time.

"The master held to his word, for he then considered you a true warrior, and he honored that. You were released, and you were granted a wish."

Guy took off the towel and looked at Matylda, and she bowed her head, as if she was grateful. She crawled up his arm and under his hair, poking her head out the other side, nesting there.

"Why don't you tell the rest, Sussy?" Guy asked me. "Her legend should come from us both."

"How can I do that?" I said. "She won't even come to my hand."

"Not yet," he said. "But you should finish her

story. Right, Matylda?" He turned his head back to her, and she nodded, just a little bit.

"I'm not a storyteller like you," I said.

"Try it with this." Guy handed me the towel. "You can do anything with this magic towel."

"Okay," I said, even though I knew it wasn't a magic towel. If I didn't try telling the story, I'd hurt her feelings, and I wanted Matylda to like me. So I covered my head with the towel, and it was dark and cozy and it smelled of Guy—the peppermint shampoo his mom bought him. It felt private in there.

"It's me in here," I said to Matylda. "And in case you haven't heard, I'm Sussy Who's Not a Storyteller. But give me a chance."

The towel helped. Words came: "Choosing a wish isn't easy," I told her, "but it was easy for you. Because you'd never been loved by anybody, and you carried with you the sorrow of fifty hearts. . . . The only thing you wanted in all the world was to be loved. It was simple.

"At the moment you were to make your wish," I said, "there was a boy and a girl on the other side of the world, me and Guy, who wanted something to love." It felt like what I was saying mattered. And

I went on. "So you lay back, you closed your eyes toward the sun, you stretched your body all the way out, from your head to the end of your tail, as far as you could stretch it . . . and you wished, wished, wished, with all that you were. You wished to be *loved*.

"Guy and you and me. Years and years of dueling for a mean-spirited future king. Years and years of our wanting something to take care of, something to love. All of it came together."

Even under the towel, my eyes were closed, and I wished for her to love me the way Guy did. The way she loved him already. I wished for her to come to my hand.

"Love can make anything happen," I said. "And when you opened your eyes, you found yourself in a tank at Total Pets, and we were there, waiting for you, looking at you through the glass. The world can be a perfect circle sometimes."

Thinking about love, I could hear my mom's soft voice, teaching me to tie my shoes, going through the steps over and over and over again on the front porch, telling me that she didn't want me to trip on my laces, that she didn't want me to fall down and

49

get hurt, and that she'd stay there with me all after-noon and the next one, too, if necessary. When I finally got it, I always made the bunny ears exactly even, just for her.

When I learned to ride a bike, later than most, Guy was there to help me, on Long Beach Island, with my parents. My dad pushed me off and I began pedaling, and then I looked down and started won-dering how I could keep my balance on these two thin wheels. Next thing I knew, I was down on the ground, and the bike was on top of me, the chain, black and oily, digging into my knee. Guy came run-ning, shouting, "You okay?"

"I'm okay," I said, popping right up, brushing off my leg. "It was nothing."

"It wasn't nothing," said Guy. He pointed to the chain marks. "Are you really okay?" My dad came over, too.

"I shouldn't have looked down," I said.

"You want to try again?" Guy asked.

"Ready," I said. And he was the runner this time, and he got me going again, fast, so fast, too fast, yell-ing, "Don't look down!" I kept going, kept pedaling, not looking down. That was the trick: Don't look down, forget you can fall, fool yourself that way.

I didn't think I was a storyteller. But Guy had helped me. Our lizard had a history now.

If Matylda had a coat of arms, it would show a savage prince and dueling lizards, but more than any of that, it would show love. Because love is what brought her to us. I believed it. She was no longer just a gecko from Total Pets. She was a warrior lizard, down to her last battle. And she'd won. She'd won for love.

Guy lifted the towel off my head and brought my hand to her. She put her starfish toes on my fingers, her gritty sandpaper toes, and she bowed, as if she was thanking me for finding my words. She didn't come any farther, but when she looked at me, her eyes reflected light, they were full of life. The three of us were the world right then.

Chapter Nine

Guy and I walked to school together almost every day once we got to third grade. He was an early riser, so he circled back a couple of blocks to get me. He told me what time the sun had risen and what time it would set each day, and the weather, too. I liked to keep an eye out for money on the ground, 'cause one time I found a twenty-dollar bill. "It happened once," I told him, "so it could happen again!"

We passed Wayne Hoffman near the entrance. He stood by the bike rack in a white short-sleeved T-shirt, no matter what the weather was. He said, "Hello, Guy. Hello, Red," every single morning, and he gave us a thumbs-up and told us what number we were.

"Why do you always give us a number?" I asked him one day. He said that after he got into a fight over a spot at the bike rack one morning, his teacher had given him a permanent place to keep his bike in exchange for a job: He had to count how many students came in each day before the bell rang and give her the tally. Even though it was just to keep him out of trouble in the morning, it turned out that he really liked saying hi to people. So we always said, "Hello, Wayne," and we thumbs-upped him back.

We had a project due, one that demanded we "look into ourselves." The official assignment was called Make Yourself Known. We were supposed to find a way to show the class something unique about ourselves, something people didn't know—even though it was already May and we were in the last marking period. My red hair was unmistakable, and I ate Craisins and yogurt for lunch every day. Guy's mom said the Craisin rut was fine, not especially imaginative but healthy enough. That must have been where his easy way came from.

When Mrs. Bueler said it was acceptable to make

ourselves known by sharing something important to us, that it didn't necessarily have to be a personal trait or accomplishment, I felt a weight off. 'Cause that meant Guy and I could bring Matylda. Mrs. Bueler said it was fine as long as nobody touched the lizard.

"Okay if she eats a cricket for the class?" Guy asked me after school.

"If my dad comes," I said. "I'm not holding the trap." My dad agreed to help out, and just before Guy went home, we set the trap out by the rhubarb.

"MAKE YOURSELF KNOWN!" Guy called to the crickets in the backyard. And I think they heard him, because the next morning, there was an über cricket in the bottle—I had never seen one so huge. The über's eyes were beady, switching back and forth between us through the hard plastic of the bottle. Its back legs were in jumping position, and its antennae were twitching, to the right, then left. It would be hard to convince me that this cricket didn't want to change its mind. We piled in the car and drove to school. "You guys take the tank and the trap," I said, going on ahead. "I'll get the doors."

"This is Matylda," Guy said when it was our turn. "Our leopard gecko. Those holes are her ears," he said, "and she can hear everything."

"She's crepuscular," he added. "Active at dawn and dusk."

Amanda raised her hand. "Does she shed her skin?" she asked.

"Every few months or sometimes more," I said. "It'll get dull before it comes off. Then guess what she does with it?"

"She does *not* eat it," said Amanda.

"Yes, she does," I said. "She gets a hundred new teeth every four months, too."

"Gross," said Amanda.

"She's a polyphyodont," Guy said. "There's always a replacement tooth coming up next to her full-grown ones. And she hunts."

Guy held up our homemade trap. "Those teeth aren't just to look pretty," he said. "She kills her prey with them before she swallows it whole."

"She does *not*," said Amanda.

"They're going to show us," said Carter.

"How much does she weigh?" asked Mrs. Bueler.

"An ounce and a half," said Guy. "But she'll weigh a lot more after she eats this cricket."

"It's very large," said Mrs. Bueler.

"I call it an über," I said. "I hope it'll go down." Then Guy explained the trap design.

"All recycled material," he said. "Are you ready to see nature in action?"

Everybody came up to get a close look, except Amanda, who was still horrified that Matylda ate her own skin. I slid back the screen. Guy had the trap.

"Watch carefully," my dad said. He unscrewed the cap, but the cricket didn't come out. Guy shook the bottle.

"It's stuck," said Carter. "Too big." Carter was right. Our trap wasn't designed for übers.

"Outta there, big mama," said Guy. He shook the bottle again. It didn't budge. The über was as wide as the bottle's neck. Everyone watched.

"Need some help?" said Guy. "That's what I'm here for." He took the cricket by its antenna, shaking the bottle at the same time. "Come on," he said to the über. "I don't want to pull your antenna off." He tugged gently, his fingers near the cricket's head.

"Come on," Guy said, coaxing it out. It was just a giant feeder to him. Finally, it landed in the tank, looking surprised to be there, squarely in front of Matylda. She didn't hesitate; she pounced and gulped. Her belly grew before our eyes, and one very large antenna was still sticking out of her mouth.

"How'd she fit that in?" Carter asked.

"Most lizards would choke on something that size," Guy said, "but Matylda's highly skilled."

"I'll say," Carter agreed, and I did, too. I admired her, even if it was hard to watch. In her own way, without a lot of show, she was still a warrior. She'd attacked the über, no second thoughts. It reminded me of when Guy took off to get my jacket that day. He and Matylda had that trait in common: no hesitation. Maybe that was why she felt more comfortable with him.

"She's flourishing," said Guy.

Watching Matylda eat that über, her belly bulging, didn't make me feel too good. Mrs. Bueler leaned down.

"You're awfully quiet, Sussy," she said.

"It's just . . ." I looked at the floor. "I try not to think about it," I said. "But the cricket's got no

chance to say the carrot's not worth dying for. No
chance to warn the rest of its family about the dan-
ger of the plastic bottle."

"It's not an easy thing to do," Mrs. Bueler said,
"but you're taking good care of her. I'm glad you
have Guy to help. He doesn't seem too worried about
the crickets." She squeezed my shoulders.

"This was very informative," she said to all of us.
"I think we learned a great deal. Thank you, Sussy
and Guy, and thanks to you, Mr. Reed, for helping.
Matylda certainly made herself known today."

Chapter Ten

It seemed like it was going to be just a regular Saturday field trip to Total Pets for me and Guy. A simple errand to get vitamin D3. Guy said we should dust the crickets with the powder before Matylda ate them. "D3's a trace element," he said. "It helps Matylda's body use the calcium. In the name of science, and our lizard, we're getting it!"

"Let's ride our bikes," I said. "We can go by the reservation and see more flowers." I wasn't that much of a nature person—at least I didn't pick up fall leaves to breathe in their scent or anything—but in the month of May, in New Jersey, the trees all flower; maybe that's why it's called the Garden State. My favorite was the saucer magnolia, with blossoms so big you could drink out of them.

"Great idea," Guy said. "I love spring!"

We knew the rules. Helmets—check. Shorts or capris or pants fastened at the ankle—check. We had the hand signals down, too, even the one for stop.

I've gone through all the things I didn't know about that regular Saturday field trip so many times. I've gone through all the things I can't say out loud. Like that the Airedale on the corner of Witchett and Elm would find the door open and come after me on my bike as I pedaled the same way I pedaled on any other day. Like that Guy, the bravest boy I knew and my best friend, would stand up to the Airedale to stop the attack, blood running down my leg. Like that the car, coming up over the hill on Witchett, wouldn't know that there was a ten-year-old boy in the middle of the road, hollering for that dog to go back, charging that dog to save my life . . .

That I'd hear the brakes squeal not in time. That I would see Guy there on the road, his body laid out, unfamiliar. Flashing lights, car doors opening, slamming, voices, terrible, terrible voices, a stretcher picking me up . . . sinking, sinking, sinking below,

below the voices, below the lights—shutting out the sound, shutting out the world.

That I'd wake up in a hospital bed, narrow, with wheels, and say, "Where's Guy?" That the nurse wouldn't answer. That no one would answer, and I'd scream "Where's Guy?"

That I'd be wearing hospital pajamas with one leg cut off, with teddy bears in little tan circles against pink cotton, gauze around my leg. That I'd scream, "Bring me my clothes my red capris and my sunflower shirt give me back my clothes I want my clothes!"

And that my mother, Ivy Reed, would come to my bed and lean over—hollow eyes, small mouth, red lipstick—she'd lean down to me, her chest and arms collapsing into me, no sound. Then I'd know that the boy who was my best friend, the boy I spent all my days with, the boy I loved more than anything, was dead.

We'd be like that for a while, me and my mom, silent like morning dew, and then she'd start humming—only chords, rocking with me like we were one. It began to hit: Guy was dead because he wanted to save me. It came to me, fast, like this, over and over and over again: Bicycle spokes. A ferocious dog running off a porch. Running to me, and me going down. My friend, jumping his bike, standing like Bigfoot with his arms overhead, with his arms overhead higher, with his arms overhead lunging and roaring at that dog, who ran back to his porch in fear. The car that couldn't stop, the noise of the crash, the car that killed the one person in the world who meant more to me than anybody else.

Guy was dead.

"Stay strong," my mother whispered to me then. "Stay strong." She pulled me in, her body swaddling me. I was on a hospital bed with wheels and pink teddy-bear pajamas, gauze wrapped around my leg, and I wasn't strong. The dog barking over and over again, the forever-long horn blaring, blaring, blaring, it would never stop blaring . . .

Blackness.

Chapter Eleven

I don't remember coming home. And I don't know how many days went by or who came and went from my bedroom. I know that the gauze came off and went on and came off and went on over and over again. I know that my mother wrapped it tighter than my father—and after one, two, three days, a week, I don't know—the gauze came off for good and a small square bandage was all that remained.

"I want my clothes," I told my dad. He had come to feed Matylda. "Where are my clothes bring me my clothes BRING ME MY—"

He grabbed my hands. "It's okay," he said. "I can get your clothes." He squeezed. "Take a breath," he said. His voice was calm, but his eyes were afraid. I'd never seen his eyes like that before.

"Do this," he said. He took a long breath in, still squeezing my hands. He let it out. "Take the air in slowly, let it out the same," he said. He took another long breath, and I matched him with my own. The air gently filling my lungs and going back out made it seem as though everything was on pause. . . .

"It helps," I said to my dad, and he sat with me then, his hands still holding mine, his wanting-me-to-be-better eyes still there. "Can I have my clothes?"

A little while later, he brought me my red capris and my sunflower shirt, and he kissed my forehead. "Here they are," he said, "all clean." My dad went to the door and said again, "Remember to breathe." He let me be then.

I had my clothes. Slowly, I unfolded the shirt—the shirt I'd had on when my best friend died. I felt the soft cotton, smelled the laundry soap, hugged it to my body. The Dying Day shirt. I put it on then, and I picked up the pants, the Witchett Road pants—somebody had stitched them up for me, tiny perfect stitches, fire-engine-red just like the pants. It must have been my mother.

There alone on my bed, I held the pants close, the ones I'd had on when my world went black. I sat with them, smoothing out the wrinkles, ironing with my hand. Then I slid my legs in, taking care.

I know that somebody gave me a Bible and somebody made me an oil painting, a vase with daisies in it. These things were on my bedside table. Daisies—still, pale-yellow center, white petals. I didn't need to count the petals to find out if Guy loved me or not. He did, and he left me here in this bed with a Bible and a painting and a lizard and a house full of whispering and murmuring. All we wanted was to see some flowers that day, to ride our bikes, to get the D3, and now he was gone.

The days came and floated in and out, and my blinds were open and they were closed, and I lay in my bed and I wanted to go to the boy I loved, I wanted to go to Guy, to follow the path of my friend. I wanted to stay close to him, and I groped my way through my dreams looking for him, to find my way to him, but he wasn't there. I couldn't find him.

Then I'd wake and see my room again and feel the bandage on my leg and know that I couldn't change my mind. That I couldn't tell him we didn't need the D3 and that Matylda was just fine with the crickets and her little bowl of calcium and that we WE NEVER SHOULD HAVE GONE ON THAT BIKE RIDE and I couldn't change it and I couldn't change it and I couldn't change it. If I hadn't been on my bike that day, Guy wouldn't have gotten off his. He wouldn't have left me here on this earth in this room in this bed wishing I was with him or that he was here with me.

Blinds up blinds down he was there and I was here.

Chapter Twelve

Then it was time for the service. I was supposed to say good-bye.

And everything was grey as I walked to the service for Guy, as I walked behind my mother to the car, step by step by step. Everything was grey as I sat down in the back of the Honda. Everything was grey as my feet touched the rubber mat on the floor of the car. I turned, looked out the window.

And everything was grey as the shapes and houses and trees and road signs of a town I knew so well, a town where I'd lived nearly all of my life, a town where there was a man who couldn't stop for Guy, who didn't understand that my very own warrior was there in the road, impelling an enemy dog to back away with his own hands. Everything blurred on that drive to the service for Guy.

My parents took my hands, and I shuffled into line behind them. The coffin was small, like Guy, like me. But the person in it didn't look like him. I swallowed hard. Guy wouldn't want anyone to see his face patched together like this. Why had they left it open? It wasn't my friend's face. And his hands were crossed over his chest. He hadn't done that in all the years I knew him. He was a saying-hi kind of friend; he should have been waving. Guy had his own clothes on, a Cougars T-shirt and sweats, and his glasses were in his hand. They got that right. But the rest was all messed up.

I put my hands on either side of the coffin, and I moved in, up on my tiptoes, close.

"Let me in," I said to him.

Nothing.

"Let me in," I commanded, right up by his face. It would be better to go with him. "LET ME IN!"

And Guy answered then, clear and strong.

"You can't come in," he said. "You've got to live for Matylda."

I knew it was Guy answering. I'd know that voice anywhere—it was the voice of a boy who saved my life and lost his own. It was the voice of a boy who wanted to see the flowers blooming with me, who wanted Matylda to get the proper nutrition. It was the voice of a knight, of someone who would miss the bus to get my jacket.

And for the tiny little time that I heard it, my world was in color again, and Guy was in his Witchett Road clothes, and it looked like nothing had happened. I saw the denim of his jeans and the white-grey threads of his ripped-out knees, and I saw the orange of his polo shirt and the blue of his Converse. His green socks, too. His favorite green socks. I saw him, and his beautiful face was not messed up.

He looked at me. "Promise me," he said. "Promise me you'll love her like I did, enough for us both." That was Guy. His demands were to the point. We were supposed to love her together. She was ours.

I couldn't give her enough for us both; she wouldn't even come to my hand. I looked at him there, still not messed up, still Guy, long brown hair, shining eyes, wide face, no freckles, glasses in hand—and I knew that I couldn't say no, and I couldn't say good-bye, that I had to hold on to him, had to say yes. I put my mouth right by his ear.

"I promise. I'll find a way to love her like you did. I promise."

I touched my heels on the floor then, touching down a few times, feeling for the surface. It would hold me.

My dad's arm around my shoulders led me away. And I think they were there, but they were like silent actors, on a stage: Mr. and Mrs. Hose, Amanda, Carter, Mrs. Bueler. . . . The only thing I knew for sure was my promise to Guy. I had to love Matylda like he did. Enough for us both. She was all I had left of him. I had to do everything right. If I did everything right, I could hold on to Guy.

Chapter Thirteen

The grey days settled in after that—one after another they came. They floated in and out, and the aloneness of me and Matylda seeped in. We were here by ourselves, and the boy who loved us was gone. How could I love her like he did?

She was in the tank, just three feet from my bed, but it was hard to get up, as mornings became afternoons became evenings became night, the promise I made a shadow, always with me. I'd said yes to stick with my friend.

The last week of school passed by as the aloneness crept deeper. My mother went back to work, but before she left in the morning, she checked on me.

"I've got clean sheets," she said. I stood up while she changed my bed, pulling the corners tight. "Could I wash your clothes?"

"Not today," I said, hands snug in the pockets of my red capris.

She smoothed out my bedspread, then perched on the edge. "You doing okay?" she asked me. "You . . . you're in here so much. . . ."

"I like my room," I said, rocking back on my heels, hands in my pockets still.

"All right," she said, reaching out to me, touching my hair. "Okay. I'll see you tonight." She touched my hair again and left for work.

There was so much to say and there was nothing to say. I chose nothing. Guy was gone, and I was supposed to love the lizard he'd left behind enough for us both. Nothing was okay at all.

My father kept bringing in the crickets. "She's not eating much," he said to me one morning. "You know what might help?"

"What?"

"If you feed her. I think she wants you to feed her."

I looked at Matylda, really looked at her, for the

first time in so long. She was thin. She must have lost her appetite when she realized Guy wasn't coming back. Maybe my dad was right; maybe if I fed her myself it would make a difference. I could help her. I didn't want to handle the crickets, but I would if it meant she'd eat. Just had to think of them as feeders, like Guy said.

"I'll try."

"It can't hurt," my dad said.

"Not hungry?" I said to her after he left. Her eyes were dull. "I don't blame you," I said. "But you have to eat. Guy would be upset if he knew you weren't eating." She was listening.

"I know what—I'll make you a deal," I said. "If I'm brave enough to bring you crickets, then you have to eat them." She didn't agree, but she didn't disagree. Maybe it would work.

Barefoot on the grass, I walked toward the rhubarb patch, where we'd caught the comrades, where he'd told me they were only feeders. . . .

I was all . . . by . . . myself.

We bought Matylda together, we gave her a story, we fed her and cleaned her tank and cared for her. She was ours, and it wasn't supposed to end like this; we were supposed to be in it together. Guy, my friend who said, "Enter If You Dare Make Yourself Known Eat and Flourish."

He wasn't here.

Just a door left open and an Airedale . . . and it had changed forever.

Guy knew how I felt about the crickets. If he were here, he would help me, just like he did with her identity when I was afraid I couldn't find the words. But no one was there.

I was on my own, and I couldn't bring him back.

In the nested soda bottles, there were two cricket comrades, medium size, who'd fallen for the lure. They would fit out the neck of the bottle. I didn't want them to get a good look at me, didn't want them to blame me for their fate, so I held the trap behind me as I carried it upstairs. I could feel the crickets jumping around inside, even from behind—and then I thought of Guy again, telling me not to look down when I was on my bike. *Don't think about it,* I told myself. That was the trick.

"Two feeders for you," I told her. "For you from me. I did it myself." I pulled back the screen top, held the bottle, and unscrewed the cap. *Don't think about it.* I shook it quickly and the crickets shot out and I closed the screen as fast as I could. The cap had fallen in, but I could get that later.

"Now stalk," I said to her.

But she didn't try to hunt them. She just sat there.

"You don't want my crickets?"

She sat.

"We made a deal," I said. "Why won't you eat?"

She watched me.

"I wanted to see the flowers," I told her. "Is that so bad? I wanted to see them with Guy." And I was back on Witchett Road and the car was coming and coming and coming and I couldn't stop it. I couldn't go back and make it not happen. I couldn't walk instead of ride, and the spokes started *spinning spinning spinning spinning inside my head, screaming, spinning spokes spinning faster FASTER FASTER—*

Breathe.

I could hear my dad. *Remember to breathe.* And I took a breath, long and slow and deep, and the world paused. . . .

Slow down, spokes.

And the spokes slowed down.

"Do you think you can love me?" I asked as she sat there not hunting. She didn't look up.

"How do I do this?" I said. "How do I get you to eat?"

Matylda came over, still not eating the feeders but looking at me, questioning me.

"I need your help," I said. Her eyes stayed on me. "Please," I said, meeting her gaze. "Tell me what to do. I need to know what to do."

At the table with my parents, I pushed my fork around my plate, because it was my first summer in five years, half of my life, without Guy, and I didn't want food—I was like Matylda that way. There was nothing to do that would change anything, but a silent meal was worse than talking.

Fortunately, we had the cricket traps.

"The evidence is mounting," my dad said. "Baby carrots may be sweeter than apples. I catch more crickets with them."

"I don't believe it," I said.

"The crickets like them better," said my dad.

"You mean," my mom added, "that baby carrots attract more crickets. That doesn't necessarily mean they're sweeter."

"They probably like the color better," I said, joining in again, saying something. But it was hard to keep up, because the color of carrots was orange, and orange was the color of Guy's polo shirt, the one he had on. . . .

I looked down at my plate and didn't look up, 'cause they might see my head full of spokes *spinning spinning spinning . . .*

Spokes, go away. Go on. GO GO GO GO GO GO GO GO GO GO GO GO so loud in my head—

BREATHE! I commanded myself.

I didn't want my parents to know how loud it was—

I breathed, long and slow.

Stay down, spokes STAY DOWN!

Now talk.

"Maybe we should try figs," I said. We had a fig tree on the deck. They turned deep purple when they were ripe.

"They'll love figs," my dad said. "What a good idea. Who couldn't love the fruit that makes Fig Newtons?"

"Then the cricket might taste like figs," my mom said.

"A fig-flavored feeder!" I said.

"And we can try pears," my dad added. "Let's do pears, too."

"And avocado," my mom said.

"We must do pomegranates," I said. "They've got antioxidants."

"We're in search of the best cricket bait!" Dad said.

"I think it's going to be pomegranates," I said with a Tic Tac smile, my perfect little white teeth all in a row. "What do you think, Mom?"

"I think you were right about getting the lizard," she said. "It's good for you to have something to love right now."

Those words brought me back to the day we discovered the hole in Mrs. Hose's theory. The day we were playing Monopoly. Mom walked right into it with her words. I looked at my plate again, 'cause I knew my dad remembered too; he would take his cue from me. Mom adjusted her scarf. None of us said a word—we couldn't. Guy's chair was empty.

"May I be excused?" I said.

"Of course, Sussy," my mom said. "Yes, of course."

There was hardly a mark left on my leg. "They're healing up from the inside," my mom said when she came to say good night. She looked at my puncture wounds, which were barely raised above the skin anymore. "That's how they're supposed to heal." She patted my leg. "Might not be a scar at all."

And what I didn't say was that there should be a scar, just like Matylda's spots. A scar would mark the day that Guy left me here to love a lizard who wouldn't even eat my feeders.

"I've got to find a way," I said. "Got to keep her strong."

"I love you, Sussy-girl," my mom said, kissing the top of my head, turning off my light. She hadn't called me Sussy-girl in forever.

Her worry was everywhere.

Chapter Fourteen

That night, I dreamed I was in a Hula-Hooping contest. There were supposed to be lots of us competing—it was a national contest—but the only contestant was me. I was in an enormous stadium that could seat fifty thousand people, and the ticket holders filtered in, ready to cast their votes. Their ballots were shaped like hearts, scissor-cut red valentines; and as the stadium filled up, the spectators waved them in the air—happy hearts welcoming me.

The price for a ticket was high, but the show was sold out anyway. Everybody got one vote, either for me or against me. If they were for me, they handed in their ballot; against me, they kept it. No scores, just for or against.

The crowd focused on me, by myself, in the middle of it all. In my red capris and sunflower shirt. The trick I was supposed to do was Walk the Dog. I knew it well. If the crowd voted for me, then I could love Matylda enough because I'd have all the hearts—so much more than I needed.

Roll away, flip my wrist, and the hoop rolls back. *Roll away, flip, roll back.* I went over it in my mind. *Roll, flip, roll back.* Easy. I could do this. It was one of the first tricks you learn in hooping. My chance to get the votes. The hearts were waving. They could be mine if I just did the trick.

Stay calm, smile, no pressure. Effortless.

They'll vote for me, I told myself.

Calm, smile, and LET'S GO GO GO GO! And I rolled and flicked and there in my dream, my hoop became thousands of hoops *spinning spinning faster rolling toward me spokes appearing shiny spinning steel*—they were bicycle spokes coming to *crush me crush me crush me.* "Guy!" I screamed.

"GUUUUYYYYYYYYYYYYYYYYYYYYYYYYYY!"
And I woke myself up with my cry and Guy wasn't there and the dream wasn't real but he still wasn't there and I couldn't walk the dog. . . .

I saw Matylda then, in the corner of her tank, the sun starting to come up. Her tail was curled tight around her head.

"I'm sorry," I said to her, getting out of bed. I couldn't stand to see her like that, in the corner. "I had a bad dream," I said. "I didn't mean to scare you. Come on over here. It's okay." But Matylda didn't move. She lay there as if she were back in the holding cell and I was the puny future king.

She'd won her fiftieth duel, and her wish was to be loved; I was supposed to be loving her, and I had scared her into the corner.

"I'll do better, Matylda. I won't scare you again."

She looked up, uncurled her tail a little. Maybe she understood that bad dreams come; maybe she was having them too.

Chapter Fifteen

I stayed there for a while, watching her, and Matylda uncurled her tail all the way and stepped up to the glass; she put her toes against it and nodded quickly, a few times in a row. "You understand about bad dreams, don't you?" She nodded again.

"Or are you just covering up?" The gecko manual said that geckos would try to mask outward signs of illness because sick-looking animals were singled out by predators looking for an easy meal. She couldn't hide the fact that she wasn't eating, but maybe she was hiding something else.

"Can I look at you?" I said. "If you're sick, I have to know." I put my hand on the carpet. She didn't come over.

"I have to check you," I said. "You don't have to come to me, but just stay still." I consulted the manual.

Eyes: Matylda's were not cloudy. Okay.

Nose and mouth: Clean.

Hip bones: I couldn't tell if they were sticking out or not, so I had to get her to move. "Can you do this?" I said, and I walked my fingers across the dresser in front of her. And she walked, too—she was helping me. "Thanks for doing that," I said. Her hip bones were not sticking out.

Wounds, lumps, or discoloration: None that I could see. But I couldn't be sure. What wounds, lumps, and discoloration did she have that I couldn't see?

She was thin, but her tail was as plump as it should be; the fat stored inside it would help her in case of famine.

If she was sick, she was good at hiding it.

"Cherry pie!" my dad called up. "Cherry pie for breakfast!"

My dad had cherry pie. "Cherry pie for my piggy!" he hollered. Guy always loved Cherry Pie for Breakfast Day at our house.

I didn't want cherry pie.

But I went downstairs 'cause he'd bought it for me.

"You still love it?" he asked. The wanting-me-to-be-all-right eyes were there. The wanting-me-to-be-all-right voice was there. The wanting-me-to-be-his-piggy was hovering over everything. So I scrunched up my nose and made my piggy face, and I said yes. He stuck a spoon in his pie. That was how we did it. We each got a pie and we each got a spoon. I used to take a spoon and a cherry pie and have no mercy.

I wanted to be his piggy and vanquish the pie. But I couldn't eat cherry pie with a spoon anymore and I dreamed that I was attacked by thousands of spinning bicycle spokes and I had scared Matylda into a corner. I had scared myself.

I didn't want cherry pie.

But I didn't tell my dad that. It would hurt his feelings, and I might see his eyes afraid again. When he handed me my spoon, his face was bright and that was good. He talked about how cherry is the best, and I dug in.

The spoon went through the filling slowly, touching down on the bottom. I turned it toward me, the spoon heaping with dark sour cherries. I could do this. I could do this without Guy. I put the spoon in my mouth, and the cherries sat there, filling me with sour and sweet, so much taste and too much taste. I held my lips together; it had to go down.

Lips still together, I saw myself, alone, in a cemetery made of screams. This was what it was like to eat cherry pie without my best friend, cherries turning to ash in my mouth, hard to swallow, dry and dusty, hot. . . .

I thought about Matylda and her crickets, of me watching her not eat. Of course she wasn't thriving. She must have felt the same way I did trying to eat cherry pie. I had to get her food that wouldn't remind her of him. We needed new flavors; maybe that would help; maybe then she'd come to my hand.

"Dad," I said, once the pie went down. "Can we try new bait for the crickets like we talked about? I think Matylda would like that."

"You bet," he said. "Absolutely!"

Chapter Sixteen

"Let's make our list," my dad said after we took our dishes to the kitchen. "We're going to buy the best cricket bait!" He had a pencil and paper.

"Pomegranates," I said.

"Kiwi," he said.

"Pineapple and mango."

"I'll raise you one," said my dad. "Papaya!"

"How about this?" I said. "Blueberries!"

"Great idea!" Dad said.

"I wonder what's going to win," I said. "I cast my vote for pomegranate."

"We can do several traps at once," he said. "An experiment."

"Why not?" I said, imitating my mom, and that's when I heard my dad laugh for the first time in forever. It was worth almost anything to hear him laugh like that.

"ShopRite?" he said, still laughing.

"ShopRite," I said. "Now."

"Yes," said my dad. "We have fruit to buy. Cricket bait!"

"Not sure about avocado," I said once we got to Shop-Rite. My dad picked through them.

"Why not?" He said it this time, in my mom's voice, and he got me. It felt like the laughs I hadn't laughed since Guy died burst out of me, as if they'd been dammed up and now were let loose.

"Yeah, why not?" I said back, once I could speak.

My dad was laughing again, and he looked relaxed. He looked younger. "I'll get everything else on our list," he said. "You do the cricket bait."

My shopping was funny—at first. I tossed a pomegranate in our cart. "Why not pomegranates?" I said.

"And why not papaya?" I laughed, putting one in.

"Why not bananas?" I got louder and threw some in. I kicked the cart forward. "Pears?" I hollered, grabbing some. "And why not apricots?" We had forgotten apricots. "HOW COULD WE FORGET APRICOTS?" I screamed. In they went. I was pushing the cart faster now, through the fruit displays.

"BLUEBERRIES! I LOVE BLUEBERRIES! I'LL TAKE TWO!

"AND KIWIS—I CAN'T FORGET KIWIS!" I screamed louder. "I ALMOST FORGOT THE KIWIS—I NEED CITRUS. WHY NOT GRAPEFRUIT AND ORANGES AND TANGERINES? WHY THE—"

That's when I saw them staring at me, every customer in the produce department, as if the voters from my dream were there, the ones I couldn't do Walk the Dog for, the ones who kept their ballots, who didn't give their hearts to me. They all turned back to their produce when I stopped and looked at them, back to their shopping, searching for iceberg lettuce, weighing their bananas, making sure they weren't plantains, smelling the parsley. Was it parsley or cilantro? Chives? Green onions or scallions? Everyone was busy.

Did they know I was the girl who wanted to ride bikes and see the flowers that day? That I was the girl who loved the saucer magnolia? That I was the girl who was with the boy who died on Witchett Road, the boy who was trying to save my life, the boy who had gone away but made me promise, even in death . . .

I was furious at Guy then, furious that he asked me to love the lizard like he did when I didn't know how. Furious that he had to get the D3 that morning. Furious that Matylda didn't love me, that she wouldn't even come to my hand, wouldn't eat my crickets. Furious I had to see the flowers. Furious I loved him so much.

I wanted to do it over, and I couldn't do it over. And the spokes came *fast, faster, faster, spinning spinning spinning* . . . "Help," I said quietly, bent over the shopping-cart handle.

Guy, help me. Where are you? Where are you, Guy? Help me, help me, please, I said to myself, trying to breathe, as I pushed my cart through the squash, the turnips, the onions. "Help," I whispered, my cart a blur of colors—all the produce in the world, and I didn't know if it was enough.

Keep moving, roll your cart, it's rolling, you're breathing. . . . Okay.

Calmer now, and I was back on Long Beach Island, on the beach. We had our umbrella and chairs set up, red-and-white-striped towels. It was especially warm, the kind of day when all the clear old dead jellyfish disks were floating on the surface. I didn't want to go in the water; even though their stingers were long gone, I didn't like the squishy jelly disks. I was scared of them. Didn't want to touch them.

"But they won't hurt you," Guy said. "They don't bite." He ran to the shore and picked up a few to show me.

"See?" he said.

"Get them away from me," I said. "I don't like jellyfish."

"They're innocent," he said, "and squishy." He started juggling them. "Don't be afraid," he said, juggling closer now.

"Guy! Stop! I don't like them."

"Touch one," he said, holding it out, wanting me to try. "I promise they won't hurt you." He wouldn't give up. He came closer. "Please just touch one," he said, right up next to me. And I took the jelly disk from his hand and I whirled it right at his face. It hit him on the forehead. He was surprised, and I was, too. He crouched on the sand, head between his hands.

"Why did you do that to me?" he said, looking up. "I just wanted you to touch it."

"Did it hurt?" I asked.

"Yes."

"Well, you hurt me too," I said.

"Really?"

"I told you I didn't want to touch the jellyfish."

"But—"

"I'm not a jellyfish toucher, okay?"

Guy looked sad then, sad that he had done that to me, and he said, "Sorry, Suss. I just like playing with them. I'm sorry."

I crouched down beside him, and I said, "Me, too. You can be a jellyfish toucher if you want. Just not me."

"You don't have to be one," he said. "I like you no matter what."

I didn't mind jellyfish days after that. I was

hardly ever angry with Guy, and we got through it okay. Maybe we would now, too.

Breathe.

My dad came back after a while. The onlookers were gone, and all my dad saw was a fruit-and-veggie shopper who'd filled her cart. He admired my produce. "I like your enthusiasm," he said. His words were warm. I hugged him around the middle, my face on his belly.

"Oh, Daddy," I said softly. "I hope this works. I hope she knows I'm trying. I hope she'll eat." My dad put his hands on both sides of my face and tilted my head up.

"It's going to work, Sussy Reed," he said. "We're going to catch the most delicious crickets in the state of New Jersey!" He put his arm around my shoulder and we moved to the checkout that way.

We got busy making more cricket traps at home. There were ginger-ale bottles to collect and cut, caps to unscrew. Bait to insert. Best locations to be determined.

"I'm going to catch you the tastiest crickets

ever," I said to Matylda that night. "You can choose your favorites. They'll be different from the ones Guy and I caught for you."

She came to the glass, and I knelt down. "I had a bad day," I said. "And I had to eat cherry pie, but it didn't taste right without Guy. I figured you might feel the same, so I'm making you different-flavored crickets. They'll be easier to eat. I'm trapping them with all kinds of produce. I think it's going to be great," I said. "Just you wait till tomorrow."

Chapter Seventeen

"Suss!" my dad called the next morning. "You coming down? Let's see what we caught. We'll see what produce worked best!"

"Dad," I said when I got downstairs. "I want to check myself. I'd like to bring Matylda something she can't resist, just from me. Let me do this, okay?"

My dad searched my face. "Are you—?"

"Yes," I said. "I want to do it myself. You're supposed to be writing a book."

"You sure?"

"I'm sure."

"Okay, boss," he said. "I'll get to work. You check the traps. Keep track of the numbers. How many crickets we caught with what kind of bait. In the name of science."

In the name of science. Dad didn't know those were Guy's words, some of the last ones I heard him say. How I hoped Matylda would like the flavored feeders; how I hoped she would like me, too. How I hoped I could do right by her, feed her and love her . . .

I took a box of mason jars, and I punched some airholes in the lids. This was how I'd keep my feeders organized. Everything would be perfect. I found my parents' jelly labels and I stuck them in my pocket, along with a pen. The first trap I checked was the kiwi, one of the baits my dad suggested. Four crickets. They shot into the jar from the trap, and I screwed the lid on fast. I was getting used to not thinking about the feeders—*don't think about it.* I wrote KIWI on the label and set the jar on the deck. Pears, papaya, and pomegranate were next. The crickets were swarming the pomegranate; I especially hoped she'd like that one. There were a few on the pears and papaya, too. Three more jars to add to my inventory.

On to the citrus, the oranges and grapefruit and

tangerines. Those traps were all empty. I made some notes. Was it the location or the acidity? I'd have to move them somewhere else to find out. The blueberries and apricots were very popular, and the crickets in those traps seemed larger. Dad would figure out why.

I had nine jars lined up in the kitchen, all labeled with their lures, the citrus still empty.

"Dad," I called. "You won't believe it!" He came up from the basement. "No crickets in the citrus traps."

"Seriously?"

"Seriously," I said. "Nuts. But look how many we caught. I can't wait to see what she likes best."

"You are your mother's daughter," he said, smiling at my neat row of jars. "I like the way you've organized this. But about that citrus, I'm nonplussed."

"Dee-dee-do-do-do," I said. "We don't know crickets, it's true. Dee-dee-do-do—"

"DOO!" said my dad. "Who would have known?"

"I'll see what she wants," I said, taking all but the empty jars up to my room.

"Are you ready for something different?" I asked Matylda. "I caught these just for you."

"Shall we try the pomegranate first?" I said. "It's very healthy." She didn't nod, but I still thought she might like it. I pulled back the screen and dumped in a pomegranate cricket, quickly screwing the lid back on the jar so the others wouldn't escape. Matylda didn't move. The cricket was jumping around, playing on the carpet, as if it knew she wouldn't bother it.

"Not your taste?" I said. I had to figure out what she liked, which meant I had to get that cricket back out before I put the next one in. Otherwise, I wouldn't know who was who. Dad would do it for me in a second, but I wanted to show her that I could take care of her. So I went and got an empty mason jar, pushed the screen back just a little, enough to drop my arm in and trap the cricket. I wasn't as fast as the cricket, so it took me a while. It seemed like every time I got close, it popped up like we were playing Whac-A-Mole.

"If you let me catch you," I said to the cricket, "I'll let you go free."

That worked.

"I'm new to this," I told Matylda. "But I want to get to know you and figure out your taste. That's why

I'm doing it." She watched me. "Now what should I try next?" I asked. "How about blueberry?" She shook her head.

"I don't have any citrus, but I've got kiwi," I said. She shook her head no again.

"Pears?" No. "Apricots?" No.

"Papaya?" No.

"Listen," I said. "He's gone, and you might not love me, but I'm in charge of feeding you now. I promised him I would. I didn't catch all those crickets just for fun. I did that for you. There must be something you want."

She opened her mouth. . . .

"What is it?" I asked. She was waiting for something. She kept it open, as wide as I'd ever seen it.

"What?" She was still waiting. There had to be something I hadn't tried. . . .

"Fig?" I said.

She nodded, three times in a row. "Fig! You want fig, don't you, girl?"

Fig! I had to get her fig! The fruit that makes Fig Newtons! "I don't even have to go to ShopRite for that," I said. "We have them on the deck."

I'd forgotten our figs, and they were ready to

pick. I ran downstairs and called to my father. "Dad," I said, "she wants figs! Matylda wants figs. She nodded three times in a row!"

He came up. "Her wish is our command," he said. And together we picked a plump, juicy fig right off our tree. My dad laid it on the counter and we sliced it down the middle, in even rounds. It had a thin skin and was purple-red inside, with a green outline shaped like a heart and full of teeny, tiny, tender seeds.

Matylda, the warrior with heart, the one people talked about up and down the mountain, the one the mean-spirited future king honored—no wonder the fig was her choice. I set up the trap right away.

"I hope we catch some," I said. "I want her to eat and flourish!"

Those were Guy's words; he wanted the D3 so she would flourish, so she would grow up and be strong. We'd dust the crickets with it . . . and then that terrible Saturday morning came blazing back, the spokes on fire, hard to breathe, and I . . . I . . . I . . . wasn't going to let them in.

Down, spokes! You can't destroy me. You're not going to win this time.

And the spokes went down.

But Guy's words stayed with me—eat and flourish. According to the manual, the D3 would ensure these yard-caught crickets were nutritionally sound. I had to get it. It was as simple as science, a supplement to the calcium I kept in her tank—wait, not tank, I meant vivarium. Had to remember that. So many things to remember to make everything perfect for her. I still had the D3 money—it'd been through the wash a few times, but it was still in one piece.

Chapter Eighteen

"I'm going for a walk," I told my dad.

"You are? That's great," he said. I didn't mention Total Pets because I wanted to do this myself. I didn't go along the road that would lead past The Intersection. I took Kermit Road. When I got there, Mike said, "It's nice to see you. Sussy, right?"

"Yes," I said. And I felt like I was doing it right, finally getting the powder that Guy was set on, hoping he knew somehow he could check it off his list. I was checking it off mine.

I felt like a ten-year-old girl with big red hair and freckles that never went away, just a girl with thin arms in red capris and a white shirt with a sunflower on the front, beige Vans. Mike could help me find what I'd come here for.

"How's your gecko?" he said.

"Kind of hard to tell. She seems to be doing pretty good, but I think she needs D3."

"Absolutely," said Mike. "Best to be safe. It's right here. Just dust her food with it." He handed me a small plastic bottle.

"You feeding her anything else?" he said. "I mean, besides crickets?"

"Uh, not really," I said. "Should I?"

"Variety's nice," he said. "You can't replicate what she'd find in the wild, but there are plenty of worms she might enjoy. Might be good for her."

"Like what?"

"Well," he said, "for starters, we've got superworms. They're over here by the crickets. They'll last three months with no refrigeration." Mike led me to the cricket box. There were stacks and stacks of yogurt-size tubs on top.

"What makes them super?" I said.

"Their size." He picked up a container and took off the lid. Each superworm was at least an inch long and as thick as a pipe cleaner, with little pointy needles on the head and a hard outer shell. "These make a good meal," Mike said, "and this shipment just came in. See how fast they're moving?" He stuck his finger in and the superworms wiggled and stretched and flopped.

"Only one a day," said Mike. "The shell's tough to digest."

"How would I feed them to her?"

"With your hand," said Mike. "That's simplest. But tweezers are fine, too. Chopsticks even work!"

"I don't know," I said. "They're so big."

"We do have daintier worms," he said. "Mealworms."

He took me to the supply room, which was really just a large closet with a refrigerator inside. You'd never know they kept worms in there. Mike opened the fridge, and there were dozens of tiny plastic containers.

"Want to see them?" he said. He opened a tub, and these worms were much easier to look at, kind of like inchworms.

"These go down easy," Mike said. "Tasty for their size."

"That sounds good."

"They'll live for several weeks. Just try to keep them cool."

"How many would she eat?"

"Depends what else she's getting," he said. "How big is she now?"

"Already six inches."

"She's the one with all the dark spots, right? You got her with that nice kid with the glasses?"

"Yes," I said. "He asked me to take care of her while he's away."

"I can help," said Mike. "Let's see . . . she could grow to eleven inches. Three or four of these a day if she's not getting anything else. But check out these waxworms." He pointed to another stack of larger tubs. "They're the fatties."

"Fatties?" I said.

"Dessert," he said. "She can't live on them, but they're—"

"Young man," a customer called to Mike. "I need assistance." She probably thought me and Mike were just friends talking.

"I don't really want a pet," she called over, ignoring her kids who were rapping on the aquarium she held. "We're just going to get a few fish."

"They always do that," whispered Mike. "They take a few fish for their kids, and they're back in a week 'cause the fish died. Nobody takes care of them. You wouldn't believe how many people want their thirty-seven cents back."

"Young—"

"Good choice," Mike called over. "I'm just finishing up with this customer."

"Back in a few," he said to me.

"We have some low-maintenance varieties," I heard him say . . .

And that's how I found myself in front of the mealworms and waxworms, alone, eyeing all the white containers stacked up in the fridge. I was thinking about Matylda, about how clearly she told me that she wanted a fig-flavored feeder. I couldn't wait for her to try it. She was beginning to trust me, and I wanted to give her more, more than just D3 sprinkled on her feeders. I wanted to give her all the food she could possibly eat! That's what Guy would have done. But I didn't have enough money for the worms.

Then I heard a voice whispering in my head, saying, *Why not take them? It's easy as pie. Just take the worms.*

I couldn't just take them.

And I heard, *Sure you can—it's okay. Show her your love: bring her worms. Guy would want you to. He'd want her to have the worms.*

Maybe I could just take them. Guy would want her to have the variety.

Yes, the stealing girl said. *It's okay to take the worms. She'll love you for it.*

"You sure?"

Yes. Love her with worms, lots and lots of worms. You can take them, you know.

Then I watched my hand, taking a tub of mealworms, dropping it in my tote. It felt good.

She's gonna love the mealies, the stealing girl said. *She's gonna love you!*

Maybe she would!

Get some waxworms too—she'll want dessert. She deserves something sweet. She needs a treat! Get her the fatties. It's okay!

Then I watched my hand, picking up a tub of waxworms, dropping it in my tote. It felt wonderful. Matylda should have a treat.

You're doing it, she said. *That's right. You can love her that way.*

I felt like I could. Matylda would be so happy to have these—she hadn't gotten anything like this when Guy was here. She'd get fresh, wormy variety in her diet, fresh, wormy variety brought directly to her vivarium by me. I couldn't wait to see her eat. I couldn't wait to see her flourish.

Fresh wormy worms—you've got them now, the stealing girl said. *That's how you do it. That's right. Go back to the crickets. You're just hanging out.*

I went back out by the crickets.

Mike was still with the fish lady. *Now take a tub of supers,* the stealing girl said. *She'll love those, too.*

"Really?" I said. "Not too big?"

Nothing's too big, nothing's too much, she said.

And I watched my hand, so confident, as it took a tub of supers and dropped them in my bag. All this variety, better than what Matylda could find in the wild! It felt so good.

That's how you do it. Mike won't know. Hang out for a bit—that's what you do. Look at the crickets. They're right there, you know.

I looked at the crickets. It was a feeder factory, hundreds and hundreds of crickets crawling around and over each other in a big black dungeon with a screen on top. They were much smaller than the ones we caught, lighter-colored too. Our crickets were very dark, and these were a dull brown; they'd probably never seen the sun. They weren't good enough for Matylda.

Mike came back then and put his hand on top of the dungeon.

"What do you think?" he said. "Pretty crowded. But it works."

My hand was on my tote, and I wasn't afraid.

"I'm glad we catch our own," I said.

"Well, if you're ever in need, you know where they are. All set?" he said.

"Yes, just the D3 today," I said. "I'm gonna stick with crickets for now."

"Sounds like a plan," he said. "There's a lot to consider with worms." I bought the D3 and left, patting my tote, patting Matylda's worms, feeling good. I had something special for my lizard.

I wanted to go right upstairs when I walked into the house, but my dad was there.

"Nice out, isn't it?" he said. He didn't notice my tote bag.

"Yes," I said. "I got D3 for Matylda!"

"You went to Total Pets?"

"Yeah."

"Well, good for you!" he said. He was glowing. "We'll dust the crickets before she eats them."

"Exactly," I said. "I'm going to show it to her."

Before Guy died, my dad was usually at his desk in the basement, writing his books, with an occasional visit upstairs and an occasional game of Monopoly. But now he was there at the door to greet me every time I walked in, even if I just went outside for a minute. If I told him that I wished he would go back to the basement and work on his writing because I just stole three tubs of worms and I had to find a place to hide them, he'd be very worried, and that would be worse than having him standing there whenever I came inside.

Back in my room, I took the containers out of my bag. "You've got choices," I said to Matylda. "What do you want first?" She came to the glass, and I leaned in. "How hungry are you?" I said. "Hungry enough for a super?" She blinked a few times when

I said that, kind of like Morse code, so I opened the container. That was another amazing thing about her—she had movable eyelids—but she had never blinked Morse code to me. She was making my job easier with her willingness to communicate.

The supers were so big and brown and stripy and crackly, and they moved quickly in the container of bran. But at least they didn't jump around like the crickets—I could pinch the end of one with my fingers, like Mike said. It flopped like a freshly caught fish, but I held tight, and I pulled back the screen and offered the worm to Matylda. Without hesitating, she came over and grabbed it.

I felt her teeth on my finger—they were tiny and pointy, and her bite caught me off guard. "OW!" I said, but there wasn't any blood or anything; it was just the surprise of those little teeth we'd talked about in Mrs. Bueler's class. They were very real. Matylda watched me, the worm hanging out both sides of her mouth one second and vanishing the next.

"Does it have flavor?" I asked.

She shook her head, confirming there was no flavor. It was all about the texture; she probably loved biting into that crackly shell. "It's the shell, isn't it?" I said. She nodded. I was glad she was talking back now, too, letting me know about the figs and the super, showing me when she was scared.

She let her tongue out quickly, twice in a row. Her water dish was full, so I knew she wasn't thirsty. She was thanking me for the worm—I knew it.

The stealing girl was right. I felt so good.

"There's more where that came from," I told her. I held up the plastic containers. "These are all yours," I said. "You shall never be hungry." I patted the tops.

I'd keep them in my shoe boxes. It was cooler in my closet. Those boxes were very important to my mother. She loved buying me shoes, and every time she brought a pair home, she stacked the box on my shoe shelf. "Unless you wear them every day," she said, "leave the shoes in their original boxes. They won't get dusty, and they'll retain their original shape." I always thought it was silly, but now I was grateful to have a place to keep my worms.

I took my winter boots out and put them in my pajama drawer. It was only July, and I wouldn't need them for a long time. Then I put the worm containers in the empty box, and I showed it to Matylda. "Your pantry," I said. "Everything you might possibly want is right here."

If a lizard could smile, then Matylda did. Her jaws went horizontal, full of teeth, a jack-o'-lantern grin. I caught myself making a jack-o'-lantern back. "We have a little secret," I said, laying my hand in the tank. "A pact. Let's keep these worms between us." She came over to my hand then, and I held it steady, hoping, hoping, hoping she would climb on.

And Matylda climbed on, gingerly, tentatively, to see if it would hold, the same way my heels felt for the floor at Guy's service—touching, touching, making sure it was really there. I held it steady for her, and her skin felt coarse and cool, her funny starfish feet like little clamps on my hand. I watched her, she was unsure but sure, too; she didn't take a step, but her toes held on. She was staying. I'd stolen the worms for her, and she liked them . . . and then she climbed onto my hand.

Chapter Nineteen

"Let's check the fig trap," I said to my dad the next morning. We went outside.

"What do you know?" he said as we got closer. "We have a winner!"

"Everyone wants to feed the warrior queen," I said, seeing all the crickets in the bottle, gathered around the fig. I brought it right upstairs and emptied the trap into her tank. She stalked, and she pounced, and she ate and she ate and she ate—Matylda was born to hunt! I knew she couldn't possibly be masking any signs of illness with that appetite.

"I think you like the triple *f*'s," I said to her. "I think you like the fig-flavored feeders very much." She nodded, a big one from top to bottom, agreeing.

"I'm so glad you told me what you wanted," I said. "Yes, I am, Matylda with a *y*, Matylda with a *y* for *YES!*"

I went downstairs for my own breakfast, and me and my dad ate together.

"I know what the *y* in Matylda's name stands for," I said.

"What?"

"It stands for *yes*," I said. "'Cause she loves figs! I've never seen her eat like that."

"She's a picky one," he said. "But she knows what she likes."

As we stood up to clear our plates and my dad headed into the kitchen, I saw an envelope on the floor under the mail slot. Somebody must have dropped it off—there was no stamp—and it had my name on it. It was an invitation to Carter's birthday party, written in green marker on a piece of lined white paper, folded in quarters.

I sat down on the entryway rug, my legs under me, the invitation in my hands. Carter was having a zombie-theme party; instead of bringing a gift, you could dress for the occasion. If Guy were here, he'd probably spray his hair with green dye and glue Ping-Pong balls on his glasses.

He'd had his own birthday party, last fall—his theme was airplanes, and he wore an aviator hat. Each of us got one, too, with sewn-on goggles and a Velcro fastener. Guy turned ten when most of us were still nine, 'cause he had an early birthday. He loved to make paper airplanes, and he had a contest at his party, everybody flying the planes they made off the deck to see whose went farthest.

When Guy's plane took off, it went up and up and up and then dived down, curling around, the fanciest flight of them all—but not the farthest. Carter's plane went farther, even though he used a stapler to make it.

After he lost, Guy went through the flight motions with his arm, over and over and over again, trying to figure out what he did wrong. He couldn't understand it. It was nine months ago, but it seemed like yesterday. I could still see him, flying an invisible paper plane, motioning with his arm, Guy of the Mystery Defeat, still puzzled that he didn't win. I didn't want to go to a birthday party without him.

My dad came out of the kitchen. "Whatcha got?" he asked. I couldn't hide the invite from my dad, so I handed it over.

"Do I have to go?" I said.

"Zombies!" said my dad. "Dress for the occasion."

"I don't want to go," I said.

"You don't have to," my dad replied, "but you can borrow my zombie tie if you want. It might be fun to see some people."

"You want me to, don't you?" I could tell.

"Only if you think you can," said my dad. And when I heard him say those words, I wanted to do it. It was safe in my room, with my butterfly mobile and rooster rug and Matylda, but I had to go to Carter's. I didn't want to worry my parents.

"I'll go," I said. "But I'm not wearing your tie."

"Roger that," said Dad. "I think you'll have fun."

Maybe he was right. Maybe it would be fun to see people.

∗   ∗   ∗

When I got to Carter's the next weekend, everybody was in the backyard already, and his mom greeted me and said, "Have you played zombie tag before?" I told her I had, which was true—we used to play it on the playground sometimes . . . but that had always been with Guy.

Whoever the zombie tagged became a zombie, too, until finally, there were just a ton of zombies and one person left, the winner. You had to outsmart the others, just like Matylda did on the mountain, fighting her last battle, fighting for her freedom and a wish. Remembering her, I wanted to win—maybe I could get that, too.

"INCOMING!" yelled Carter. He was the zombie. And then I felt like lightning on the grass—I had to win. Like Matylda, I weaved and I swerved and I ducked, a snake on the lawn; nobody could catch me. Flattening myself behind a tree, I peered around.

One, two, three, four zombies now—five of us left.

And I was a cheetah, fierce and fast, leaping over rocks, ducking behind bushes, crouching in the corner behind the garage, outwitting my opponents, time after time after time. Sneaking, creeping, on the edge, five, six, seven zombies now . . . zigzag jumping side to side, behind the pond—zombies circling, one boy standing . . . till he was a zombie, too.

Just me then, in the middle, hot . . . breathless, the winner. . . . But I wasn't on the mountain; I was in Carter's backyard, surrounded by eight zombies, sixteen eyes watching me . . . they were zombie eyes, and they were growing bigger and bigger and bigger . . . and I was scared, and the eyes grew legs—getting longer, growing growing growing they were giant round eyes with long black legs marching toward me closer, closer . . . closing in . . . circling circling tighter tighter closer closer closer—*STOP! RETREAT! GO BACK! GO BACK! GO BACK! GO*—

"SUSSY! Are you okay, Sussy?" Carter's mom asked. She was right by my face, gently shaking my shoulder—her mouth so close I could see the spaces between her teeth. "Are you okay?"

I looked at her. Then I looked around the circle. The marching eyes . . . they were gone; the giant round eyes, the eyes with legs closing in on me—they weren't there anymore. It was just Carter and the others, watching me, looking at me, waiting for me—

Breathe.

And I breathed, long and slow, in and out, the way my father showed me that day in my room when I needed my clothes.

Breathe.

Now talk.

"I'm okay," I said to Carter's mom. "I was just . . . just . . . out of breath. Had to rest. . . ."

"Of course you're out of breath. You ran so fast. You won the game, Sussy! You won!"

Carter's mom clapped, and everybody joined in. I was the winner. She put her arm around me. "You get to be the zombie now!"

I couldn't be the zombie. I was afraid of the marching eyes that weren't there anymore. They might return. I didn't want to see those eyes.

I backed out of the circle, away from her, from them, from my fear. . . . One foot, the other foot, turning forward, faster now, going going going going away from the zombies—Carter's mom calling me, once, twice . . . her voice fading out, my feet keeping going.

My dad was at the door when I got home. "Already back?" he asked. "How was it?"

Answer. Don't tell him about the marching eyes.

"I won zombie tag," I said. "But I didn't feel like staying."

He knelt down, my height now, eye to eye. "You went," he said. "That was brave." Then he whispered, "And you won the game without even wearing my tie." He was trying to be funny, but I didn't feel funny.

When I got upstairs, I went to Matylda. "I swerved and ducked like you," I said. "I was the last one standing. But I didn't get to make a wish—"

I stopped talking then, because there, on the windowsill, a ladybug landed, touching down as if Guy and I were on the watch again. I hadn't seen one since he died; maybe it meant some good luck was coming—big luck or little . . . it might be coming.

"Matylda?" I said. "Do you think you can love me, even if he's not here?"

I put my hand in the vivarium, flat against the carpet.

She came on and moved closer, onto my wrist, looking at me, touching me, maybe saying yes . . . and I felt a little firework go off inside, a tiny sparkler lighting up, from my belly straight to my heart.

"Can you feel it?" I said. She spread her starfish toes. "Can you feel the sparkler?"

Chapter Twenty

We'd been going to Long Beach Island the first week of August since I was little, every single summer, and Guy had come with us the last few. We rented the same house every year, one back from the ocean, in Beach Haven. So when my parents told me it was that time of year, the time for some sun and sand and corn dogs and gelato, and they said they knew it would be hard to go without Guy but we were going to do it together, I knew that I didn't have a choice.

I didn't want to go to Long Beach Island without him. I didn't want to stop at Lucille's for chocolate-covered pretzels and maple creams without him, and I didn't want to go on the Drop Zone, either. He wouldn't be beside me when the ride dropped down, with no warning, again and again and again. He wouldn't be beside me for corn on the cob or steamers; he wouldn't be there to show off his three-step husking method or tell me to watch him drown his steamers in a pool of butter.

I didn't want to play Yahtzee without him. I learned the game at our beach house, and I taught it to Guy. He thought the dice would give him what he asked for, so he always brought them right to his mouth and whispered, "I have faith in the dice." If we somehow rolled a Yahtzee—five of one kind—we had to do a dance. I ran like a deer and did split leaps; Guy turned into a wild turkey, flapping his arms and waddling around, right on the beach. I'd never get to see him whisper to the dice or do another Yahtzee dance.

"Then I have to bring Matylda," I said to my parents.

"Oh, honey," my mom said, "we can't bring a lizard to the beach. The owners won't—"

"I have to bring Matylda," I said again, louder. We were in the living room, and my mom came over then and sat next to me on the red couch. "I have to bring Matylda," I said, flat and loud.

She put her arm around me. "Honey, you—"

"Don't touch me," I said, standing up. "I have to bring her." I backed away from my mother, toward the stairs. "She's coming," I said. "I won't go without her." I was in reverse, going backward up the stairs, holding the banister. "You can't make me. You can't make me!" I was calling down from the landing now. "I won't go!" I went into my room, and I picked up the vivarium. "It's not too heavy!" I yelled down. "And she only needs water and food. She won't make a mess. She's coming with us. Tell me she's coming with us. She's coming, she's coming—"

My mom appeared in the doorway, me standing there, vivarium in my arms. My feet stayed planted as she moved toward me, holding out her arms to me and Matylda. And as she took the tank from me, my arms were jelly . . . I felt so tired. "Yes yes yes yes, Sussy-girl," she said. "Yes, she can come. Of course, she can come."

She set the vivarium on the bureau, and I went to her, so tired, so tired from holding the tank in my arms, so tired from trying to go on, from trying so hard to go on without my friend, from having to go on without him. "Promise?" I whispered. "'Cause I won't go without her, Mom. I can't go without her."

"I promise," she said. "You don't have to go without her. Yes, she can come." And she laid me down on my bed and tucked my covers around me, and I closed my eyes . . . so tired.

We went a few days later, me and Matylda and my parents—her vivarium next to me in the car, its own safety belt buckled. My dad left the crickets in the soda-bottle trap with a few extra figs and brought the whole thing along. The crickets could eat the figs during the week and we would feed Matylda when she was hungry. I packed some worms, too, just in case—I wanted her to have the same variety at the beach that she now had at home.

I unpacked my duffel and looked at her there in the same twin bedroom I'd shared with Guy. It came to me then that she'd never know what the beach had been like with him unless I tried to show her. I could do that.

So I said, "Let's go! Let's uncover the secrets of the ocean!" I put on my swimsuit, the same suit as last year, a navy-blue Speedo, built for exploring the water.

"Let's bring her to the beach!" I said to my parents, who had their suits on, too. Faster than a jack-in-the-box, my dad was carrying the vivarium across the ramp that led over the dunes, with me and my mom behind, the beach mostly empty in the late afternoon of a cloudy day. I chose a spot near the back, and my mom laid out our blanket. My dad set the vivarium down in the middle.

"Do you like the ocean?" I said to Matylda. "Do you see the waves?" She shook her head.

"Can you hold her up so she can see me swim?" I asked my dad.

"It would be my pleasure," he said. He looked happy.

And running into the water, I submerged my whole self at once—the cold was easier that way. I looked back, and my dad was walking toward me at the shore, vivarium in his arms. My mom was coming in too, up to her knees, getting used to the water inch by inch, like always.

"WATCH ME, MATYLDA!" I yelled. "I'M A FISH!" I dived through a wave, popping out the other side, jumping up, showing her my hands, then diving through again. "I'M A FISH!" I yelled, frothing about, showing her my fins. My mom had reached me now. "WATCH THIS!" I yelled to Matylda, even though she couldn't hear—she'd know it was for her. And me and my mom held hands, and we rose up over the wave, so smooth, and up again over the wave.

And then I jumped on Mom's back, remembering how she first taught me to swim in the ocean, showing me everything was okay, even when the water crushed me and went up my nose and out my ears. It was salty and good and fresh. "Here we go!" she said, and we rose up together, and I was high on her back, waving to Matylda, still there in my dad's arms.

"THIS IS HOW YOU DO IT!" I yelled. "WATCH!" My mom and I bodysurfed in, our timing perfect, riding on the water right up to the sand, right up to where my dad was standing.

He was so strong, still holding the vivarium there, and my mom was so strong with me on her back. I felt so strong too, and proud, showing Matylda the ocean the way Guy would have done.

"Your turn, Dad!" I said. "Put her down, and you

go in!" I sat with Matylda, on the blanket, while my parents swam. They loved to go way out and swim together.

"Did you see me?" I asked her. "Did you see me be a fish?"

She got onto her log, right before my eyes, and she wiggled off.

"Are you being a fish?" She did it again.

"You are," I said. "I have so much more to show you! The docks and the sunset and the water park." I thought of Guy and what he would have done.

"I'm going to show you the moon tonight," I said. "How it hangs over the ocean, and I'll tell you the story of the astronauts who landed there."

"Listen," I said to her, quieter now. "Listen to the waves. They have their own rhythm. Can you hear it?" And as we listened there, I remembered how Guy would call for me, beckoning me out to the sandbar to jump and ride the waves with him. And the thought filled me up because even though I missed him, I was doing right by him and Matylda. Pounding waves on the shore, the rhythm of summer, of me, of Guy, of my parents still swimming out there, and of Matylda now, too.

"Do you hear the pounding?" I asked her. She looked at me and nodded. "The ocean," I said. "It's pounding for all of us." I felt close to her.

"Can I pick you up?" I asked. She lifted her belly, just a bit, so that I could get my hands around her. She was letting me pick her up. I brought her to my face, careful not to squeeze too tight.

I closed my eyes and made a wish then, with her in my hands, so close to me. I wished for her to know, with every single pounding, that I'd take care of her like Guy did, that she was safe with me, that she could trust me, that we'd get through. That I couldn't bring him back but we'd get through.

Chapter Twenty-One

My mother knocked on my door when she got home one night, not too long after Long Beach Island. She carried a shopping bag full of new clothes.

"For a change," she said, brushing the front of my sunflower shirt.

I wasn't going to change my clothes. I didn't want to wear something else; my shirt was what I had on the last day I was with my best friend—this shirt and my red capris, neatly stitched around the tear.

"Listen," my mom said. "I know it sounds silly, but sometimes a simple change on the outside can make you feel new." She set the big shopping bag on the floor. "I know you love that shirt," she said. "With that big sunflower."

"That's not why I like it," I said.

The room was quiet for a moment.

"It's just . . . well, look," she said, holding up a turquoise shirt with a frog on it. "Have a look. Think about it. Look at this embroidery." Underneath the frog it said BULL.

"And it's very funny," she said. "A bullfrog!"

And then I was back with Guy, on a field trip at school, a hike we took at a nature conservatory. Guy fell behind the group, and nobody could find him for a while. The chaperones were concerned, and then we all heard, "CAWOOOOOOHAH!"

"That's him," I told everyone. "I'll get him." And I ran to Guy, who was standing by the stream, not on the trail, gently poking a giant bullfrog with a fern.

"Come back," I told him. "Everyone's looking for you." I grabbed his hand and he gave the frog one last little poke, and it sprang off its rock and made a joyful splash.

I smiled at my mom then. How did she know I'd like this silly shirt, that Guy would have liked it, too? I grinned.

She kept talking. "Shorts to go with it," she said. She held up the shorts, celery green, and I was still thinking about Guy, missing him but smiling too. "What a nice complement to the turquoise," she said. "Land and sea."

The frog shirt made me happy, remembering people trying to find Guy, and he didn't even notice, too busy watching that frog, with its big belly and strong legs that could send it so high in the air. No wonder Guy loved frogs.

My mom kept talking, on and on. "And wait till you see this skort. Now, I know you're not a fan of skirts, but a skort . . . you can do anything in this." I nodded, my mind in the air with Guy and the frog. I felt so happy, thinking about him and that trip; I felt like I was up in the air, too!

"Celery may be the trend," my mom said, "but purple never gets old. And this cherry top. These sleeves," she said. "Not really short, not really cap. Just right. And overalls! They're back. New jeans, too. I didn't go too nuts," she said. "Levi's. Nothing designer—"

"CAWOOOOOOHAH!" I yelled, interrupting. "I'LL TRY THEM ALL!" I felt free. It didn't make sense that something on the outside could make me remember Guy with happiness, not sadness, lift me up that way. But it did. "Cawooooohah," I said, softer now

"Oh, Sussy," my mom said. "You will?"

"Yes," I said. "Yes, I will, Mom."

"Oh—oh, Sussy. That's good." She closed the door so I could change in private.

"Jeans first," I said to Matylda, and I put them on and called my mom in.

"They're perfect," she said, admiring her own ability to buy the right size. "You're lucky you have me. You may never have to visit a dressing room. Overalls next."

Matylda was watching me—there hadn't been so much activity in my room in a long time. I put on the overalls. They had lots of pockets.

"Ready," I said.

"Adorable, Sussy," my mom said. "Those are going to come in handy."

The skort and cherry top fit too. Then I tried the celery-green shorts and the bullfrog shirt, and I felt like running to Guy at the stream and poking that frog together. I felt so close to him right then, my fingers going over the bumpy surface of the frog on my shirt, remembering Guy and the field trip the whole while, almost as if he were with me. I went around each embroidered letter then, the smooth floss so nice, so silky.

My mom knocked on the door again. "One last thing," she said. "Sandals. You've never seen sandals like this." She brought in a pretty pair of flip-flops with decorations on the straps. "Go ahead, try them." I put the sandals on. "Fabulous!" she said. She picked up the box and headed toward my closet.

"I'll get that," I said, blocking her. What if she decided it was "passing-on" day, when she went through all my clothes and shoes to see what I'd outgrown? She looked surprised. "It's just that, well, you know, I'm double digits now, have been for a while," I said, standing in front of the closet. "And I've got to start taking care of my stuff—I mean, I'm in charge of the lizard and everything now—gotta organize my own shoes, too!" I had to keep her out of the closet.

"Did you buy anything for yourself?" I asked, changing the topic.

"As a matter of fact," she said, "I did manage to find a few things." She put on a pair of red gloves. "Clearance," she said. "Nobody wants cashmere in the summer, so I pounced."

"They're so soft," I said, feeling the gloves, feeling her fingers. She took my hands, her red-gloved ones on top of mine. She got quiet.

"You must miss him," she said.

I felt quiet now, too, my throat tightening. What I wanted to say was that I missed him all the time, and that the shirt had made me remember him with happiness, by the stream, and that was nice.

"A lot," I said.

"I know," she said. "I know." My mom squeezed my hands and let me be alone then. I put the new clothes in my drawers.

Matylda was watching from one of her palm trees. That's when I noticed she had no place to go for shade if she didn't feel like being in one of her privacy logs. "Are those palm trees big enough?" I said. The answer was clear; she didn't fit under them. "They hardly look like trees," I said.

Suppose she just wanted to feel sheltered? She needed more leaves—there was no shade. And her privacy logs were just that, logs she could lie under. She couldn't even stretch her neck under there. It all seemed inadequate. Only three leaves on each branch of her trees. I used to think her vivarium was nice, with its glass walls and trees and pool and heating pad—with its brown carpet. But it wasn't good enough for her.

"Do you like your vivarium?" I said. She didn't have to answer. Her huddling under that nearly leafless tree was answer enough. I had to do better for her. "I'll get you a shadier tree," I said.

Chapter Twenty-Two

I'm going to Total Pets," I told Matylda the next morning. "As soon as the store opens," I said. "I'm going to get you the best tree in the whole store!"

That's what Guy would have done. He knew how much I liked spring, with the flowers blooming, every color imaginable and more, and a few years back, he showed up at my house early on a Sunday morning, pulling a wagonful of tulips and daffodils.

"I got you the best flowers!" he said, grabbing them into his arms. "Look how many!" he said. It turned out he stripped his mom's garden clean, and my dad's too, just to bring me all those flowers, all those colors. My parents weren't pleased, and neither were the Hoses, but they weren't angry for too long, because it was Guy, and the flowers were for me. It was hard to stay mad at Guy of the Big Bold Heart.

Today I would wear the clothes my mom bought me and get Matylda a new tree. Today I would leave my sunflower shirt and red capris behind. Today I would put on the new bullfrog shirt and the celery shorts.

My dad smiled when he saw me. "Nice duds," he said. He didn't want to make a big deal, and neither did I.

"Could I get her a new tree?" I said. "Do you mind? I think she needs more shade."

"Don't mind at all," said my dad, and he dug around in his worn black wallet. If he were a whistler, he'd have been whistling then. We finished our breakfast, and I headed out, twenty-dollar bill in my pocket.

When I walked into the store, Mike said, "Hey, you're back. I like that shirt."

"Thanks," I said. "I need a better tree for Matylda's vivarium. She doesn't have enough shade."

"Shade's important," said Mike.

"Yeah," I said. "Those palm trees we got—hardly any leaves. What else do you have?"

"Lots of choices," he said. "Follow me." He headed to aisle 3.

"Look at these," Mike said when I caught up to him. "Every kind of tree she could possibly want."

"I want the best tree you have."

"Easy then," he said. He walked farther down the aisle.

"These are the rainbow trees," he said, showing me an assortment of fantastic trees, with dozens of branches and rainbow-colored leaves. "They don't come like this in nature," he said, "but geckos love them." He picked one up. "This is the same tree my bearded dragon has."

"You have a bearded dragon?"

"Yep," he said. "Monty's been in our family fourteen years. He was passed down to me by my brother when he went to college."

"Wow," I said. "Fourteen."

"With any luck," Mike said, "he'll live to be twenty, at least."

"What's your secret?"

"No secret," he said. "You've got to have proper

lighting, of course, heat, variety in the food," he said. "And this might sound crazy," he whispered, "but I talk to Monty every day. I just put him on my hand and talk. I think that keeps him going. He's a listener."

"Matylda's a listener, too," I said. "I talk to her— maybe too much."

"You can never talk to your lizard too much," Mike said. "Monty's proof." He smiled. "Oh, and I let him play, too."

"Like with an activity center?" I'd read about those.

"Informally, yes," Mike said. "Monty likes all kinds of stuff, but I don't keep it all in one place. His favorite is a hamster ball."

"Like a wheel?"

"Nope," said Mike. "Like this." He took me over to a different aisle and showed me a red glittery ball, with airholes and a removable top. "Monty runs around in this thing all the time. Keeps him in shape. He's got a lot of energy. And he stays in it when I clean his vivarium."

"But it says it's for mice, rats, and hamsters," I said, reading the label.

"Look," said Mike. "Don't just stick to the herp department. We've got a whole store here." He motioned to all the back aisles. "Get to know your lizard. Try different stuff."

"I wouldn't have thought of that," I said. "Thanks. I'm going to take a look around."

"Do that," said Mike.

There were so many possibilities. Mike was right about not sticking to the herp department—if he hadn't told me to try different stuff, I never would have considered these things for Matylda. But looking at the Silent Spinner—like a spinning stool at a diner, but with sides—I thought it might be good. There were all kinds of run-around wheels, too. Would Matylda be like Monty, running around in the hamster ball? She didn't really seem like the exercising type, but then again, you never knew.

Mike was coming down the aisle with a customer behind him. "Follow me," I heard him say. "The fish are over here." He eye-rolled me as he went by. He must get those fish people all day long. I went back to the trees, feeling the money in my pocket.

So many trees, the stealing girl said. *No need to buy one. Pocket the money—you might need more stuff.*

Savings for her. That's how you love her. Steal the tree. No one's around.

I looked around. I had the aisle to myself.

Best to have the money—she might need it someday.

It was true. Matylda should have a financial cushion, just like my dad's nest egg. Good to plan for her future.

Put it in your pack—there's no one around.

And then I took the tree, the most beautiful rainbow tree, and I put it in my pack.

Zip it up now, the stealing girl said. *You've done good work.*

I zipped the pack. I had the tree, and I felt so good, 'cause I had the money, too. I had a nest egg for her!

He's still with the fish, the stealing girl said. *You can get away, very easy today. Mike's with the fish—he'll be there for a while. Straight through the door, no one around. Walk slowly, leave the store leave the store leave the store.* I left the store, walking slowly, the tree safely in my pack.

Keep on walking, she'll love that tree. Don't look back.

Mike was right about the tree, and I was so glad I'd taken it. Because as soon as I put it in Matylda's vivarium, she climbed under it, and she looked like she belonged there. I thought she might be getting ready to shed, but I wasn't sure. Her yellow skin was the color of an old dandelion, not as bright as usual, but against the rainbow tree, she blended in so perfectly.

And as I watched her, looking glorious there under the tree I stole for her, I felt I was keeping my promise to Guy, loving her as much as he did. Doing just that. Sussy the Promise Keeper. I had the money, too, just in case she needed something. And I wanted to do more. I wanted her to have everything! I wanted to love her more.

"Dad," I yelled. "Come look. Matylda loves her new tree."

"It suits her," my dad said, walking in.

"Thanks for letting me get it." Me and my dad hugged, and as he left my room, everything was just as it should be—my new outfit on, my mom at work, my dad writing, and Matylda with a new fancy tree and some just-in-case money. I closed the door, and she raised herself up again, like she had the first time she let me pick her up. We had a secret signal now. So I put my hand around her belly again and I placed her on my palm.

"I'm glad you like the tree," I said. She was listening. "I stole that for you. That's how much I love you. You can count on me." I paused then. "I've got savings for you, too," I said. "In case of emergency."

I think she understood, because Matylda, of the ancient face and starfish toes, began to crawl up my arm. I watched her, afraid to move, and I felt her—tiny, tickly, scratchy steps, going up, one after another after another. Her little toes, grabby on my skin, teeny wondrous grippy feet. Matylda crawled, all the way to the top, and she settled behind my neck, the same way she had settled behind Guy's when we first brought her home.

"You walked up my arm," I whispered, turning my head toward her. She was lodged there against my skin. "Stay there," I said. And I sat, head straight, a statue—like Guy had done. I wanted her to stay.

"Do you see us, Guy?" I said. "Guy? Do you see? Is this what you meant?" She tightened her starfish toes on my neck. "See, Guy? Is this how you did it?"

We sat there together for a while, her soaking in

my body heat, feeling close with her under my hair, and then I placed her back under her new tree.

Her vivarium looked like a luxury hotel, and she seemed pleased to be in it, under the most spectacular tree you could get, knowing she had worms from Total Pets, fresh fig-flavored feeders from our yard, and just-in-case money.

Chapter Twenty-Three

Why *not* celebrate new beginnings?" my mom said when she came in the door from work that night.

"*Why not* celebrate with sushi?" my dad said, sweeping the takeout bags from her hands. They must have planned it, to celebrate my clothes. I wanted to celebrate too. I joined in.

"Attention!" I said. They both looked at me. I cupped my hands around my mouth and shouted, "Why not?" They were laughing now. We were a silly family of why-notters...

"Howdee-doo, *oshinko*," I said, taking the sushi out of the bags. "Howdee-doo, yellow radish roll!" I took out more food. "Hello there, Mr. and Mrs. Tempura," I said. "Good evening, little shrimp dumplings. Oh, right, excuse me. Good evening, *shumai*! *Bonjour,* green dragon. But you, Mr. Uni, Mr. Sea Urchin, I have nothing to say to you."

"Pardon," my mom said. "I beg to differ on Mr. Uni." She picked up the sea-urchin sushi. "You may look like a spongy, brick-colored blob, Mr. Uni. And you taste like old cheese, but I love you the most!"

Mom plunked it in her mouth, closed her eyes, and *Mmmmmmmmmmmmmmmmmm* is what I heard.

My mom hadn't been this silly in a long time.

We sat together, me and my parents, under the chandelier, with flowered cloth napkins and chopsticks. "Thanks for getting my favorites," I said to my mom as she picked up a piece of green-dragon roll. Then, in a low voice, with my hand as a microphone, I asked, "What was the highlight of your day, Ivy?" That made her laugh again, 'cause she used to do it to me, before . . .

"Well, my dear," she began, "the highlight of my day is your—"

"It's got to be about you," I said, shaking my head. "Not my outfit."

"Right," she said, "but your outfit is terrific. Someone with excellent taste must have chosen it."

"It's not bad," I said. "Not bad at all. Now back to you."

"Highlights, hmm. Let's see," she said. "Groundbreaking day is set for Hudson River Park. You know, that's our new account. The menu's been approved—that's always my biggest challenge, the wine list, appetizers, the gluten-free sides. . . . They wanted to serve Brooklyn Lager, too, even though the park is in Manhattan. I prevailed, though," she said. "We're serving a sunset red ale brewed right in New York County."

"You didn't compromise," said my dad.

"That's right," she said. "You have to pick your battles."

"Sussy didn't, either," he said. "You should see the tree she brought home for Matylda."

"I can't wait to show you, Mom," I said. I really couldn't. "Matylda loves it."

"I'll bet she does," my mom said. "And how about you, Manny? Did you have a highlight?"

149

"I had a good day," he said. "Thanks to this one right here." He pointed to me with his glass. "And this one here." He pointed to my mom. "You ladies," he said, "you both know what you want." Glass to me again. "Suss, you wanted shade for your lizard and you brought home the best tree money could buy. And you, Ivy, with that ale. No settling for the Reed women."

"We shall not settle," I said, and I saluted them both. I knew I never would—Matylda's tree was sparkling in my mind, fluorescent and shiny and shady.

"Here's to your book, Manny," said my mom.

"No compromising!" he said.

"Never, ever, ever!" I added, clacking my chopsticks together, laughing. "Prepare for attack, *oshinko*! I'm coming in." I put that crunchy, pickly radish roll in my mouth.

"Green dragon, beware," my mom said. "I'm going to demolish you!"

"Dee-dee-dee-dee-do," said my dad. "Good-bye, *uni*." He put it in his mouth and chewed slowly. "*Mmmmmmmmmmmmmmmmmmmmmmmm*." *Uni* was one thing they both loved. I was another.

My mom put her chopsticks in the air. "To new beginnings," she said. "And new clothes."

"To a new season," said my dad.

"To bullfrogs," I said.

My parents were wishing me well; they were rooting for me. That's one thing I knew: They were cheering for me. They would vote for me, always. There was something about wearing these clothes; it seemed crazy, but maybe my mom was right, because I felt different in them, like maybe I could go on, like maybe we all could go on.

"I have a P.S.," I said.

"P.S. what?" said my dad.

I cupped my hands over my mouth again. "P.S., Dad: You gotta stop the red-purple Monopoly thing if you want to play with me again. Okay?"

"But I haven't won that way yet," he said.

"P.P.S.," I said. "You never will. Can you hear me?"

"Well, okay," he said. "Considering everything, okay."

"Thank you," I said. "Thank you berry merry mushroom." Then we all had a laugh, 'cause that was a line from *The Silly Book,* one of the books they used to read me all the time. We couldn't get enough of the stupid, silly talk, and somehow, tonight was like that too, even without Guy.

After dinner, upstairs, I said to Matylda, "Mike says I can never talk to you too much. You agree?" She nodded. "Want to come out?" I reached in and she crawled straight onto my hand. We lay together on my bed.

The lizard manual said that you can watch movies with your gecko to make them comfortable. They might sit on you to take in your warmth—you could bond that way. But it didn't say anything about lying on your bed together, talking. I guess it was about the same thing.

"I loved him," I said, "ever since that day at the bus stop. He always put his heart first, you know?" I stopped and caught my breath. She was listening. "That's how he died," I said. Matylda looked at me, her eyes serious.

"He loved you that way, too," I said. "And I want to do right by you. It's not the same anymore." Matylda crawled up my arm, my shoulder . . .

"You're all I've got left of him now," I said. "And

I'm all you've got left, so we should be a good match, now that you'll come onto my hand and everything." She was rubbing her back against my shirt, against the shoulder seam.

"You like my shirt?" I asked. "Cawoooooohah," I whispered. She kept rubbing. I reached up to her, patted her, and then her back skin was in my hand, rubbery and soft.

Matylda had shed on my shoulder.

I held her skin there, admiring the skeletal white web, perfectly the shape of her spine, the spine of a warrior lizard.

"You're not scared anymore, are you?" I asked. "You don't think I'm the future king, do you?" She didn't move, tired from her shed. She'd been that dull color for a few days, so I knew this might be coming . . . but her timing, it couldn't be a coincidence. "You want to start over, too?" I rolled her skin, fresh, between my fingers.

"You do," I said. "We're the same that way." I laid her skin on my chest, drumming my fingers on it, slowly. Then I picked her up, off my shoulder, her back so bright again, but some old skin still hanging off her face. I left it there. The manual says not to pull off any skin that doesn't come off by itself. Shedding could take a few days.

"You're ready for Halloween," I said to her, "with that side flapping mirror skin on your face." She moved her head from side to side, and the mirror skin flapped a little. "You've got a sense of humor, don't you?" She nodded then, Matylda of the Ancient Face and Side-View Mirror.

Nowhere in the manual did it say this. That your lizard might shed on your shoulder, against your shirt, just when you were starting over. Nowhere did it say your lizard could make a joke, either. But Matylda wasn't any lizard—and I would do right by her.

Chapter Twenty-Four

"I'm going to ride my bike," I said to Matylda a few mornings later, still feeling new. "I'm going to get right on it and pedal." It just came out. Matylda put her starfish feet on the glass and went vertical, like she was going to climb. I knew she couldn't—she didn't have toe pads—but she acted like she was going to try. I'd never seen her do that. "Is that a standing ovation?" I asked. She stayed in place. "No need to answer—I know it is."

"I'm going to ride my bike," I said again, this time to my dad at breakfast.

"You sure?" he said.

"Yes, I am, Mr. Reed," I replied. "It's been sitting in the garage all summer long, and it wants me to ride it."

"You don't have to, you know," my dad said.

"I know," I said. "But I want to."

I got my bike out of the garage. If I could just get my feet to push the pedals. . . . I had my helmet and the new shorts. I had on my *Cawooooohah* shirt. The tires were a little flat, so I got out my air pump and I plumped them up, pushing down the handle, up and down, up and down, quickly at first as the air went in, then slowly, heavily, harder to push as they filled.

The tires firm, I turned my bike upside down and rested it on its handlebars. It was just a simple machine, with two wheels, a chain, and a frame, and I began to turn the pedals with my hand, the hand Matylda liked now, the hand she'd crawled on, the hand that made me hopeful. Around the wheels went, around and around and around.

"Cawooooohah!" I said, to nobody and to everybody. "Come on!" The chain was still well oiled, and I turned the bike right side up, placing the tires back on the ground. Put down the kickstand.

I backed up then, took a good long look at this simple machine.

It's just a bike, I told myself. *Come on Come on Come on!* I put up the kickstand and straddled the frame. My feet could touch the driveway. Right foot on the pedal, and I began to go, very slowly, left foot now. . . . If I could take this first trip, in my new clothes . . . *keep pedaling, don't look down, that's the trick, don't look down.* . . . Around the house I went, pedaling through the arbor, past the tiger lilies, the birdhouse, the vegetable garden, the cannas—fiery-red, sky-reaching flowers. . . . Through the backyard, past the rhubarb patch, the basketball hoop, down the driveway, across the front lawn, and I did it again. Did it again and again and again and again. And again.

"CAWOOOOOOHAH!" I hollered to the world. "Cawooooooohah," I said, not hollering now, just pedaling. And then I pedaled some more; I pedaled and pedaled and pedaled and pedaled till I could hardly feel my legs, the no-leg feeling the best of them all.

I was pedaling again.

Chapter Twenty-Five

A week or so later, my mom came into my room, with a little bag in her hand. She sat on my bed and said, "School's around the corner."

I hadn't thought about going back to school. And Matylda was just getting to know me. She climbed on my hand and up my arm; she nestled behind my hair. She let me know when to pick her up, and she had given me a standing ovation. She loved my fig-flavored feeders, and she blinked Morse code. We had a secret stash of worms, a secret wormy pact, and she had shed on my shoulder. I couldn't go back to school now. I wanted to be with her; I wanted her to flourish. That wasn't possible if I had to go to school.

It wasn't okay.

"Mom," I said, shaking my head. "She's just getting used to me. I don't want to go. I can't go. I can't leave—"

"Sussy—"

"No," I said. "I have to take care of her. Please don't make me go. Please, I—"

"It's time to start over. You're doing so—"

"No. I won't leave her. I won't I won't I—"

"SUSSY!" she said. "You've been so brave," she went on, softer now. "You can—"

"No no no no no," I said. "I won't—"

"SHHHHH!" my mom said. Which made me be quiet. Because it wasn't a sound I was used to hearing from her.

"Listen," she said. "Remember how you didn't think you could go to LBI, and it turned out o—"

"She came with me," I said.

"You can't take her to school," my mom said. "It's not realistic. You've got to go back—"

And I began to cry, 'cause there was no way out this time. 'Cause I had to leave Matylda, and I had to go to school without Guy. 'Cause I wasn't ready and I had to be ready and I couldn't be ready.

"How will I do it?" I said. "I don't know how to go to school without him. I don't want to leave her. I don't think—"

"I wish I could tell you it would be easy," she said, holding me. "I can't do that. But it's only six hours a day. Something you have to do, for yourself and your future. You can do anything for six hours a day, and we can help with Matylda."

"I don't know how to go without him," I said again. "I miss him so much."

"I know," she said, moving her hand in circles on my back, slow, gentle circles, around and around. She sighed. "It's just that you can't stay in this room forever."

And she began to cry, too, and we held on to each other for a while, and there was no magic wand, and there was no eraser, and there was no pressing rewind. There was no going backward.

"We have to move on," she said. "Have to go forward." And when I heard that, I wanted to be on the saucer with Guy again, sledding, not knowing where we were going, knees tucked in . . . but I couldn't be, 'cause he was there and I was here. Sussy and Guy Not Together Anymore.

*School, without Guy, going to school without Guy.
Away from Matylda, leaving her alone, just when she'd
started to like . . .*

"I brought you something," my mom said. "It used to be mine, but I wanted you to have it. It's a little silly, but, I don't know, I just thought it might help." She handed me the tiny bag. "I'll let you open it in private." My mom closed the door behind her.

While Matylda hovered by the palm tree, I opened it. There was a long navy-blue jewelry box inside, wrapped in light-blue tissue—a silver bracelet. There was a single charm on it—and I understood. It was a brown fedora, the same one Indiana Jones wore. My mother had brought me a bracelet that would give me the strength of Indiana Jones, a magic bracelet that would help me stay strong. A magic bracelet and new clothes and I'd go to school. I had to. *Six hours a day.*

Matylda was watching me.

"Want to come out?" I said. She nodded, as if she knew our alone days were coming to an end. I lay on my bed, holding her right over my face.

"I have to go back to school, you know. But it's

just six hours a day. I'll miss you," I said, "but when I get home, it'll be better than ever. It can be like that, you know. When someone goes away it's even better when they come back." I set her on my chest. "Six hours is just three hundred sixty minutes, it's over in a flash. So don't worry. I'll come home right after we're dismissed."

Quieter then, I said, "It'll be lickety-split. I won't forget about you. Just six hours."

My mom poked her head in later that evening, on her way to another event. She was dressed in green and she smelled like lavender. "It's beautiful," I said to her, 'cause I knew she was checking about the bracelet.

"Oh, I'm so glad. I was hoping so."

"I love it," I said.

She was my mom, and she'd chosen the name Indiana to give me strength. She was my mom, and she'd given me a bracelet with his fedora on it, to help me stay strong. She was my mom and she loved me and I had to go to school.

"You look pretty," I said.

"Thank you," she said, tucking her hair behind her ear. "That's nice."

I held up my wrist and showed her how the bracelet looked.

"It suits you," she said. "It's lovely."

Chapter Twenty-Six

First day of school, fifth grade. I'd wear the overalls today, and the new sandals with gems. It was still warm enough.

"I'm going to walk to school by myself, Matylda with a *y*. Never done that before." I buttoned myself up at the waist and hooked the straps into their holders. "I'm going to miss you," I said, bending over her, looking down through the top. "Very much."

She took a drink of water, fast-forward licks from her pond. Her skin was all shed now. I still had the spine piece, and I held it up. "Okay if I carry this with me?" I asked.

She nodded, and I put it in my pocket.

"It'll keep you close," I said. She was looking at me.

"You want to keep me close, too?" I asked. "You do? Okay." I unclasped my fedora bracelet and hung it from her tree. "You take care of this today. And every time you see it, you remember we're like Indiana Jones." Matylda shook her head from side to side again, like she thought that was funny.

I waggled my finger at her. "That's not a joke," I said. "You stop that right now." I laughed. "And don't you worry, either. I won't be gone too long. Six hours."

"Breakfast is ready," my dad called up. "And I'll give you a ride."

"I'm going to walk," I said, coming down. "Gotta break in my new sandals. They've got gems, you know." He slid my egg-in-the-hole out of the frying pan.

A piece of bread, a square cut out of its center filled with egg and neatly fried. Ketchup on the side. Even though I'd had it so many times, the whole package pleased me, with the extra cutout square grilled in the same pan.

"Well, you are prepared," said my dad, browsing

through my well-organized backpack. "I don't think your mother missed anything on the list."

"I suspect not," I said. I stood up then and put my dishes in the sink, rinsed off my hands and brushed them on my sides. "No yogurt and Craisins this year," I said.

"Gotcha," my dad answered, opening the fridge. "Then it's going to be . . . meatloaf! How about a meatloaf sandwich and a side of chips?"

"Why not?" I said. Somehow that joke never got old.

I picked up my lunch bag, knowing I had to leave. "I'll be going now," I said, puffing up, feeling like a thousand doors might be opening in front of me, or that they might be locked.

"You know where to find me," Dad said. "Say the word and I'm there."

"Good-bye Mr. Egg-in-the-Hole," I said. I did a little skip step to keep it light.

I'd said good-bye, to my dad and Matylda. Nobody was circling back to pick me up. Nobody was telling me when the sun had risen and when it would set. Nobody was telling me the weather. Nobody knew I was looking for money on the ground.

Walking by myself, I was Sussy of the Sandals with Gems. *Okay, girl,* I thought. *Just a walk. Two blocks south, turn to the left. Three blocks.* With each step, Guy not here became more real. *Whistle now.* Guy taught me how last year—let's see, tongue against my bottom teeth, lips pulled in, and blow.

As I got going, the song announced itself—from Disney World. Years back, my first trip there, sitting between my parents, riding the boat through It's a Small World. Funny this song came out now, straight from the Magic Kingdom. I was maybe four when I heard it the first time, before I ever knew Guy. The song took me right back. Just me and my parents, in a boat, *whistle, whistle, whistle.* I was on my way again, in my magic kingdom with my magic clothes. The sandals were comfortable, overalls loose. Nearing the school.

Like nothing had changed, Wayne Hoffman stood by the bike rack. Same white T-shirt. Didn't know what he'd say. There was no "Hello, Guy" to go with "Hello, Red." Wayne Hoffman surprised me.

He said, "Woof."

Got my attention. He knew. And he knew that

I knew that he knew. We connected with *woof.* His way of telling me he'd heard about the Airedale.

"Yes," I said to Wayne, keeping puffed up. "I'm on my own."

"Red," said Wayne, "I'm walking you in."

"'Kay," I said, feeling a wave of welcome. So much better to walk in with somebody than to walk in alone.

Nobody else said a thing about Guy that day, and I didn't either. You wouldn't know he'd ever existed. Nobody asked me what happened, and I didn't tell them, just like at Carter's. Nobody else said *woof.* Nobody talked to me much at all, and I was thankful for that. I was moving on. I didn't have Mrs. Bueler anymore—she was from last year. It was the same school, but we were in a different wing. None of the teachers I remembered were there to see me.

"Sussy Reed," said Mr. Mujica, my new homeroom teacher.

"Here," I said.

"I'm expecting big things from you." He didn't know a thing, or if he did, he didn't let on.

I ran into Amanda in the lunch line.

"Buying hot?" she said.

"Just milk," I said. "Got a meatloaf sandwich." I shook my paper bag.

"I'm buying hot," she said. "Still got the lizard?"

"Yeah," I said. "She just shed." I grinned.

"Gross," said Amanda. The summer hadn't changed her, so I didn't tell her I had Matylda's skin in my pocket—it was drier now than when it first came off, but it wasn't brittle. It was safe with me.

Coming out of the line, I scanned the cafeteria. I hadn't thought about this—hadn't thought about lunch, my table, sitting at my table without Guy. We sat together, just the two of us, Guy with his tomato and American cheese on rye bread and me with the Craisins. Now the room was so big, so much bigger than I remembered. Without Guy, without my lunch buddy, I was like a new girl, on her own. Where did a new girl sit? Rows and rows of tables and noise and trays and voices and . . .

"RED," said Wayne Hoffman, less than a foot away from where I stood. "Sit here, Red. Sit with us." A whole new table, the boy who said *woof,* the boy who said, "I'm walking you in." That was where I sat. Magic clothes and a magic table. Skin in my pocket. I took my sandwich out of the bag.

"You're all right, Red," Wayne said. And I felt all right. As I sat there with them, I felt new, I felt like I was more than walk to school / walk home / Pringles / ginger ale / play Monopoly / or maybe Yahtzee / two square once in a while. I felt like more than all that minus Guy plus Matylda.

Now I felt like Red. This boy, Wayne Hoffman, was kind. And the sandwich wasn't bad. I'd agreed to meatloaf just to get away from Craisins, but it was tasty. Four boys at the table who were new to me.

"Doing Ecology Club?" the boy with shiny black hair asked.

"What is it?" said Wayne.

"Mostly just a place to get together," the shiny-black-hair boy said. He was Scott.

"Not doing it," Wayne said. "Not unless Red does." He looked over at me, and I looked at him. I'd never been asked to join a club.

Da-da-da-dum: Get a new suit, get a new friend, get an invitation. Da-da-da—

"Well, Red?" Wayne asked.

I smiled.

"You're gonna do it," he said.

And I said, "That's right." It all sounded fun and funny, and it was light. But it didn't feel light inside. It felt like another ocean wave of welcome, bigger now. An ocean wave of these boys wanting me at their table when I didn't know where to go. As if they caught my SOS of where do I sit / how do I do this / this room is huge. And all because of Wayne.

Da-da-da-dum hello overalls, hello Wayne, hello club. I felt like skipping rope to that tune. I felt like skipping rope forever. *Hello, Wayne! Hello, new table!*

"When does it begin?" I said.

"Two weeks," said Scott, who was on the other side. "We meet in Mujica's room after school on Wednesdays."

"He's my homeroom teacher," I said.

"Condolences," said Wayne, laughing. "My brother had him. Did he tell you he expects big things from you this year?"

"He did!"

"Then you're probably in his top five," Scott said.

"What's that?"

"The kids he counts on to score well, who bring up the average of the rest of the class," Scott said.

"That's okay," I said. I didn't mind if I was a top five. It was another sign that everything was going my way. I wouldn't have to try to fit in—I'd be assigned a table, a team. . . . *Da-da-da-dum! First day of school and the top five rule! Da-da-da-DUM-DUM-DUM!*

Yahoo hoo hoo!

Cawoo hoo hoo!

Chapter Twenty-Seven

I skip-stepped home with a *hoo hoo hoo*. An A-OKAY and a two-thumbs-up.

"Dad!" I yelled. He was pulling two boxes across the lawn. They fell to the ground as I jumped into his arms. "It was good today." I scrunched myself as tight into him as I could. "It was really okay. Wayne Hoffman was nice to me. And I was asked to join a club. Amanda Pittock hasn't changed, but I have new friends in the lunchroom." My dad held me tight.

"The meatloaf sandwich was really great," I said. "And I'm in Mujica's top five. I'm going to help his class average go up." I held my dad as hard as I could. "I did okay. I did okay."

And then we sat down on the steps, and some tears came down, because all of the fear I'd been holding inside, the magic clothes and magic brace- let and all, the thousands of doors that I wasn't sure would open, that I thought might be locked, all the worries weren't there anymore.

"Paper tigers," my dad said. "Thank goodness for paper tigers."

"What are paper tigers?"

"Things you worry about that end up being harmless."

"That's right," I said. "It was all paper tigers. It's going to be okay."

He held me there, stroking my head. It was so nice to know it was paper tigers. "What's in those boxes?" I said.

"A trampoline," he said. "So you can jump to the sky!"

A trampoline! Never would I have thought that on the day a thousand doors opened, a day of paper tigers, I would also get a trampoline. The welcome waves were twelve feet tall now.

A trampoline. I saw them there, bouncing, all the

boys from my new lunch table. Bouncing, bouncing, bouncing. Somersaulting circus tricks, laughing, clapping, having fun. A trampoline club. We could meet after school, not on Ecology Club days. We could all have Pringles and soar to the sky.

"I can hardly believe it!" I said. "A trampoleee-eeeeeeeeeeeeeeeeeene!"

"Let's set it up," said my dad. And we worked together then, laying out the ring first, connecting the metal pieces, my dad making sure each bolt was locked. Next were the springs, and as we rolled out the trampoline and started connecting it to the ring, it got harder and harder and harder. "The tighter the trampoline, the higher you can bounce," he said. He was connecting the last ones himself. I couldn't wait to bounce. Then he put on the spring protectors and he said I could jump, even though the safety net wasn't up. It was nearly dinnertime.

I scrambled up. "Spot me," I said to him.

"Ready," he said.

"Have you ever seen me jump?" I said. I got going.

"To the stars!" I yelled. Split leap. Jump, jump,

jump. "I'm a Top Five!" I hollered. Straddle jump. "Got new friends and got new clothes!" Tuck. "Had a new lunch and got a new club. Meatloaf's good and Craisins are gone."

I jumped some more, arms out to the universe. "Listen to me!" I said, looking at my dad. "There's going to be one afternoon, every week. One afternoon when I won't be home early. One afternoon when I'm in a new club!

"Now listen some more," I said. "I HAVE NEW FRIENDS!" And I straddle-jumped again. "I'M GOING TO BE O—"

"KAY!" shouted my mom, home from work, grinning at me. I jumped off the trampoline and into her arms.

"I had a great day," I said.

"Hooray," she said, hugging me. "I'm going to make you dinner—whatever you—"

That's when I remembered Matylda. I hadn't fed her; I hadn't said hello. I'd forgotten all about her. I darted inside, double-stepping up to my room. I'd forgotten my lizard. Left her alone all afternoon. She was curled in the corner. I'd forgotten her, too busy with my trampoline, too busy telling my dad about my new friends. "Matylda!" I said. "I'm sorry!" She kept her head down.

"Oh, no," I said. "Oh, no. Matylda, I don't know how—how I could have done that. I didn't even check your trap. I didn't check for your triple *f*'s." Here I was, with my overalls and new sandals, skin in my pocket, my meatloaf sandwich, my new trampoline—and I'd forgotten about her trap. I'd left her alone all day, come home and set up the trampoline.

I'd forgotten all about her . . . the welcome waves came crashing down.

I felt so small then.

Guy? Are you listening? Are you still there? I'm try-ing. But just when I get going, I fall behind again.

I ran to the fig trap. There was one juicy cricket there, sitting in the middle of the tiny seeds. I brought it upstairs. "It's just one," I said, "but it's a fat one—not an über, but a nice one. Here it comes." I watched the cricket's descent. Matylda saw it land, but she didn't stalk. Her eyes were blank, and she didn't move at all; she'd been eating so well ever since we found her favorite flavor, but she wasn't eating now. I'd let her down.

I had to make it up to her, never forget her again, no matter how many welcome waves I rode, new lunch-table friends and all. I didn't want her to feel invisible.

"I'm going to make it up to you," I said. "You don't need Guy to eat and flourish." His words had come out, just like that. They weren't only his anymore.

Chapter Twenty-Eight

I wore another new outfit to school the next day, my purple skort and my cherry top with the just-right sleeves. And even when I found out that Carter would be sitting right next to me, and that Mr. Mujica expected big things from him, too, I was thinking about making it up to Matylda. Even when I took out my brown paper bag at lunchtime with another new sandwich in it, this time turkey and cheese on potato bread with spicy brown mustard, I was thinking about her, at home, for six hours.

I had to make it up to her.

And when I told Wayne and Scott and Silas and Juan about the new trampoline, and how it had a fourteen-foot diameter and was called a JumperSportz, I wanted to make it up to Matylda. I was remembering not to forget her.

As soon as the last bell rang, I went to her—ran right home and up to my room, to my warrior girl. I picked her up and sat back on my bed, leaning against the pillow. "I was thinking about you all day," I said. "I'll never forget you again." It seemed like the peek-through yellow spots on her skin got brighter as I spoke. A good sign, but her face from yesterday—like she felt she didn't matter—I couldn't erase it.

"You're not nobody," I said. "You're what I have left." I held her, brought her to my face, up close. I had to make it up to her.

Give her a present, the stealing girl said. *That's what you can do. Get the hamster ball, the red glittery one. Make it up that way. Give her a present.*

The stealing girl was right. I could get her a present. "You want that hamster ball?" I said to her. "Of course you do, yes. I'm going to get it for you.

I'm going to get you a present." Her skin got even brighter. "You need exercise, don't you? Yes, you do. Sitting in that vivarium all day. Gotta work out. That's right. It's no trouble," I said. "I'll get you the ball."

I put Matylda back in her vivarium, and I emptied my backpack and put it on again. "I'll return," I told her. "With a present."

"Dad," I yelled downstairs, "I've got to run back to school—left my agenda there."

"Okay, Suss. You have another banner day?"

"Yeah, Dad," I said, whatever he meant. I had to get the glittery ball for Matylda. I walked to Total Pets, very fast, all the way along Kermit, turning right onto Elm. Going to get the ball.

"Hey," said Mike as I walked through the door. "Welcome."

"Hi," I said.

"How's your gecko? Still talking to her, I hope."

"She's not doing that great," I said. "She needs something, just not sure what."

"Have a look around," Mike said. "You'll know it when you see it."

"Okay," I said. He went to greet a customer, and I

went to aisle 3—the red glittery ball was there, still new-looking, still shiny. *That's a good present,* the stealing girl said. *Put it in your pack. No one's around.* I unzipped the pack and dropped it in. *That's right,* she said. I zipped up my pack.

The ball is safe, the stealing girl said. *Move through the aisle and on to the next. Have a look around. Put your hands on this, put your hands on that—you're making up your mind. Don't rush now, and you won't get caught. Pick up the Silent Spinner, have a look around. You're doing it right. Don't rush now. You've got the ball; it's safely in your pack. Count to one hundred. Count to one hundred before you leave.*

Turn the Silent Spinner—you might buy that. Take time to read the label. Would Matylda want that? Thirty-one, thirty-two. Would Matylda get dizzy? Forty-nine, fifty. Count to one hundred before you leave. Deep breath now, the ball is safe. Sixty-eight, seventy. Wait now. Count now. . . . Ninety-nine. One hundred. You can walk away. It's all okay. Walk like your backpack's empty. It's okay, Mike's nowhere to be seen. Probably getting fatties for somebody else.

Walk. Through the door and outside, walk by the carts. Walk. Through the parking lot, don't look back.

Keep going to the sidewalk and walk like your back-pack's empty. Keep moving.

Down Elm Street, keep walking. Left onto Kermit, keep walking. You're safe, just you and the ball. It's a glittery present. Matylda might love it. Open the door, close the door.

"I'M HOME!" I yelled.

"Hello!" Dad yelled back. He didn't come upstairs. Everything was good now—he didn't need to hover, didn't need to lurk.

"Now," I said to Matylda, unzipping my back-pack, "do you feel like getting some exercise?" I held up the ball. Matylda looked curious, even if she wasn't nodding. "Monty loves his hamster ball." I took off the lid and put Matylda inside.

She looked nervous in there. She put one foot forward and the ball turned—Matylda adjusted her weight, got her balance. She started going forward again and peered up at me.

"Do you like it?" I said. "Is it a good present?" She was unsteady on her feet. "Do you want to roll in it?" She just sat there. "What's wrong?" I said. "Not what you wanted?" She lay flat, and that told me every-thing. I hadn't chosen the right accessory.

They have other stuff, the stealing girl said. *All kinds of stuff. All kinds of presents. Get her something else.*

I could try something else. *You can go back! So much to choose from, so many presents.* Yes, I'd go back.

"They have other stuff you know," I said to Matylda. "What would you like?"

I had to get the right thing. What would I get? I didn't know—had to get something to make it up to her. She didn't like the ball. She wasn't answering me.

"It's okay," I said as I put her back in her vivarium. "There's more where that came from." She scooted under the tree. "You really like this tree, don't you?" I said. "You like the shade." It seemed so—I had that right. She was under that tree, on her belly again—relieved to be out of the hamster ball.

I hid the sparkly ball in a pillowcase in the back of my closet, behind my sleeping bag. The worms were starting to smell. I'd forgotten about them—she was so happy with the triple *f*'s. I checked the waxworms; they were dying—hard, sour crescents. I opened my window and dumped them out. I popped the lid off the supers—their smell was awful, rotten, old and foul, and they didn't even look like worms anymore; they were becoming beetles before my eyes. I dumped them out, too. Then I checked the mealies; they smelled bad. Threw them out. I had to get new worms.

"I'll get you more stuff," I said to Matylda. "And I'll get you new worms. I'll get you the best stuff they have."

So many presents, so many worms. Get them all for her! Make it up that way. Show her who you are!

"I'll make it up to you, Matylda with a *y*. Just you wait."

Chapter Twenty-Nine

Buy something small and take something big, the stealing girl said, waking me up the next morning. *So many presents. Get her what she wants—make it up to her. As soon as the store opens!* And I felt like it was meant to be, because it was Saturday and when we finished breakfast, my parents said they were going to Home Fixings to buy a new grill. Their timing was perfect, 'cause I knew it would take forever for them to agree on the best one.

I left the house right after them. *Yes, buy something small and take something big,* she said again. *It's easy! Retrace your steps, Kermit to Elm to Total Pets.*

"I'm back," I said to Mike, walking in.

"Hey," he said. "Busy day here. Lizard okay?"

"I still haven't found the perfect thing for her," I said.

"Well, I'm here, even if I'm swamped. It can take a while. No two lizards are the same." Mike was always helpful, never in a bad mood, even when he eye-rolled the fish customers.

Back to aisle 3, the stealing girl said, *that's where you go.* I went to aisle 3.

Unzip the pack. No one around. Drop the Spinner in—hurry up now. Take a Climber Block—she might like that. Barrel Roller too.

I was moving quickly, keeping up.

Still room left. No one around. Hurry up now! Flying Saucer Wheel, put it in your pack. Faster faster faster—Igloo too! Nut Knot Nibbler? Yes yes yes. Hurry hurry hurry! You can take it all! YOU CAN TAKE IT—footsteps, footsteps—zip the pack, zip the pack, ZIP THE PACK NOW!

"Made up your mind?" said Mike.

Heart beating fast, but you're okay. You're all zipped up. Collect yourself and talk to Mike NOW!

"Mike," I said. "I . . . I . . . I just don't know! I want to make her happy and—"

"You have school today?" said Mike.

You don't have school. Answer him now!

"It's Saturday!"

"Right," he said, "it's just . . . just your back—"

"This?" I laughed. "I've always got this thing on."

That's right—distract him from the pack!

"What does Monty like?" I asked. "I mean, besides a hamster ball?"

"Let's see," Mike said. "I guess—" He paused, looking at me. "I guess he likes the Comfort Cupboard best."

"How does it work?"

"I—I attach it to the wall of his viv," Mike said. "And Monty does the rest. He even likes Cupboard peek-a-boo."

Keep talking.

"Not sure Matylda would do that," I said. "She mostly likes eating."

"I—I just unloaded a new case of mealies," Mike said. "Maybe—"

"Oh, man," I said. "That's it. Fresh mealies!"

Buy the mealies and leave! Get out of the store! GET OUT OF TOTAL PETS!

I took the mealies and paid at the checkout.

Walk. Walk ahead. Straight no look back keep walking past the carts through the parking lot don't look—

"SUSSY!" yelled Mike, running toward me. "YOU FORGOT SOMETHING!" He had my tub of worms. I'd left them behind.

He knows, the stealing girl said. *Get out get out get out. NOW!*

"Look," said Mike, handing me the worms. "I wasn't sure what—I . . . I mean—I'm—I know about your friend!" he said. "I know what happened. And I'm—I'm sorry and . . . I'm worried . . . I know you took—"

Run run run—Mike knows what you've got! Run run run—Mike knows that you steal. Run run run—Mike knows what's in your pack! Get out get out get out get out. Run run run—he sees who you are! Run run run—Matylda needs the stuff! Run run run run RUN WITH YOUR BACKPACK NOW!

I took off then, I ran and I ran and I ran, to get away from Mike. He knew what I'd done. I ran, out of breath, backpack clanking, blew through the door, and straight up to my room . . .

And there was Guy.

Sitting on my bed, in his orange polo shirt, his jeans, and his Converse. His Dying Day clothes. Looking at him like that, thinking about him demanding that I love her as he lay in his coffin, I understood.

I'd been wasting my time.

Because I could never love Matylda the way he did; I could never love her enough, feed her enough, buy her enough, or do enough. Seeing him there, I got it. I went to him then, stuffing one of my socks in his mouth; it was good to see him like that, silent sock-mouth Guy, a paper tiger, too. It was my turn to talk.

"These are the worms I got for Matylda today," I told him. "The stealing girl helped me. I wanted Matylda to have fresh mealies—that's what you would have done." I opened the tub and poured them on Guy.

"And here is a Nut Knot Nibbler," I said, showing it to Guy. "To see if she likes to chew." I set it on the bed. "And this," I said, taking out another toy, "this is a Climber Block. I hope she likes it." Looked in my pack. "Here's a Barrel Roller," I said, holding it up.

"See how it turns?" I spun it for him. "It's meant for mice and hamsters, but she can use it, too.

"Oh, and this," I said, my voice getting louder, "is an Igloo." I brought it right up close. "I thought this might be fun in case she didn't like the Barrel Roller. You know she can be finicky—she didn't like the hamster ball I got her.

"And how could I forget this?" I asked, pulling the Silent Spinner out. I gave it a whirl. "So many possibilities," I said. "Can you believe it? I got her all these things. . . . But you know what? It's not enough. It will never be enough. I finally get it." I talked faster. "I went to Total Pets, and I listened to the stealing girl—I filled my backpack with things I didn't pay for, for Matylda, for you, for that promise. . . ."

I hated him.

I hated Matylda, too.

And most of all, I hated myself as I yanked the screen off her vivarium and threw the Nut Knot Nibbler down on her. Hated myself when I threw the Silent Spinner, right on her tail, and the Climber Block next. Hated myself, throwing the Barrel Roller in, throwing the Igloo on top.

Hated myself more as I hurled the Flying Saucer

191

Wheel, hard, like a Frisbee, right at the glass. Picked it up and hurled it again.

I looked around the room. Grabbed my comforter and covered Guy, laid myself on top of him. "I hate you," I whispered.

And the spokes came rushing back, the same ones from my dream, and I couldn't push them down—they came rushing and roaring through me, and they were bicycle spokes, shiny spinning steel, and they were coming to *crush me crush me crush me* again, and I left him there and I ran out the door, ran from the spokes if I didn't run faster they'd crush me and I ran and I ran and I ran and I ran. . . .

Chapter Thirty

I ran to Guy's.

I burst in the door, slammed it behind me, and the spokes crashed against it, waves of crashing, as loud as the car on Witchett, the driver not prepared to stop, as loud as the crash that killed Guy. I could still hear it.

I tore up the stairs to his room.

"I HATE YOU!" I yelled. "I hate you," I said, feeling the coils of his braided rug under my feet, the same rug we played on so many times, so many games, so many days—I looked around his room. . . .

It felt so familiar. Four pillows on his bed, as always. Yankees shirt, neatly folded, on the back of his chair. His mother must have done that. Paper airplanes. Skateboard, butterfly net. These things I knew. But in the middle, there was more.

The waffle iron. A dozen knitted hats I'd never seen, each with an orange base and lifesaver stripes, each the same. I picked one up, the yarn was so soft, fresh-baby soft, the same orange color as his Witchett Road shirt. I put it on my head.

I saw it all again then—Guy, jumping off his bike, charging that dog, charging that dog with his arms overhead, a knight, not worried about anything but me. . . .

His body on the road.

Bike day, long-gone Guy day, that moment on Witchett . . .

He wanted me to love Matylda, just the way he did.

But I wasn't good at doing that. I couldn't do that. I didn't do that. Guy, my best friend, who made my cherry pie taste like screams . . .

I woke up every day wishing I could do it again, wishing I could ride with him to Total Pets to get the D3, to make sure Matylda stayed strong, wishing we could see the flowers, until I remembered the car that didn't stop, the car that couldn't stop in time, the forever-long horn blaring. . . . And then I was right back there on Witchett.

I got it—I was always gonna be on Witchett somehow, was always gonna hear that crash—loud or quiet I'd hear it. I was supposed to hear it; it was part of me. Okay, dying day, you can stay.

I sat there with my hands on the hat, feeling the softness, holding myself. I missed him so much. I loved him so much.

My voice came then, a whisper, riding on air, a message going out.

"I can't do it your way, Guy; I can't keep my promise. Will you stick with me anyway? Do you hear me?"

"Do you want waffles?"

I looked up. Mrs. Hose was in the doorway. "I heard the noise," she said. "I didn't know who it was." She stood there, her face, her eyes, her arms—full of so much love, so much sorrow, so much missing.

She'd lost him too. . . .

"I'm glad you came, Sussy," she said. "So glad it's you."

I went to her, and she folded me in.

"This hat's so soft," I said. "I've never felt a hat so soft."

"Blanket yarn," she said, pulling me tighter. "I knit those," she continued, "hoping . . . hoping somehow he'd know I wanted to keep him warm—"

I started to take the hat off; she'd made it for him, not me.

She pushed it back down. "You keep it," she said. "He'd want you to have it. He'd want you to stay warm, too."

"I'd like to wear it," I said.

We were hardly breathing, hugging so close, just the two of us—her terrible emptiness and her enormous love, right next to mine . . . and I burrowed in deeper, our feelings all together now, my world bigger with her.

Loosening our hold after a while, I picked up the waffle iron. "You want to have waffles?" I asked. "I think he'd like that."

"That child," she said. "He never did tire of waffles."

I brought the waffle iron downstairs, and Mrs. Hose started mixing up the batter. "How hungry are you?" she asked.

"Very hungry," I said. "So hungry."

Mrs. Hose put the waffles on the table, with syrup and butter. But she didn't set a place for Guy, only for the two of us.

"He'll find them," she said. "He knows where they are."

Chapter Thirty-One

$\mathcal{I}$ finished my waffles and went home, to my room, pulled the comforter off my bed, the comforter I'd used to cover Guy. There was nobody there. Nothing there but worms.

I went to the vivarium, but I couldn't see Matylda under all the stuff.

Gently, I began taking things out—everything I'd thrown in—carefully, slowly. When I got to the bottom, there, underneath it all, lay the warrior who'd won fifty battles, the warrior of the ancient face and starfish toes. Matylda of the Bright and Tender Skin. She'd dropped her tail. The manual said that lizards dropped their tails to throw off predators, because the dropped tail wiggled around as if it were alive, and the lizard could fool the enemy and have time to get away. But Matylda hadn't gotten away.

Standing by the glass, I watched her, with her little tailless body. Her stump.

I was the predator.

The stump was hard to look at, and I could only think about how I'd treated her. All she wanted was to be loved—that was the wish she made after her final battle. I'd tried to love her the way Guy did; I'd tried to love her enough for us both. And I failed, and I ended up hating her and hurting her, ended up hating and hurting Guy, too.

Minutes going by, standing there, speechless, staring, knowing she'd lost her tail at my own hand, remembering and not remembering. I'd buried her alive in mouse and hamster accessories, buried her alive, nearly killed her, came close, so close.

And as I watched her there, without her tail, I could feel my heart—it was getting so big—so big with love . . .

I wanted her to live.

I wanted her to live and live and live and live and live!

We could grow up together, her and me. . . .

Not everybody got to.

I picked up her tail, held it in my hands, no longer part of her. My hands, capable of so much destruction.

I didn't hear my parents come in.

But there they were, in Matylda's mirror, coming toward me. . . .

I couldn't escape.

Set my eyes on the tail.

Could feel their fingers on my shoulders.

Couldn't look up and couldn't turn around— could feel their eyes . . .

On the tail, on the toys, on the tank.

On the worms.

On me.

They could see everything.

Breathe.

And I breathed, long and deep . . .

Now turn.

I turned, my eyes meeting my mother's and then my father's—one to the other and back.

Their eyes—afraid and confused and alive . . .
fierce and brave and ready . . . their eyes were fear,
their eyes were hope, their eyes were love . . .

They were my eyes, too.

I reached my arms around them, and I could feel
my dad's breath as he let it go, a stream of air—

Then the doorbell rang, several times in a row,
and someone was knocking.

"I'm off my shift!" Mike hollered. "I figured out
where—"

I threw the tail on my bed and ran downstairs,
as fast as I could, had to get to him first. My parents
didn't know how I got the stuff. I opened the door.

"Please don't tell! PLEASE DON'T—"

"Hey," he said softly, stepping back. "It's okay. I
just stopped by to make sure you're okay."

His kindness took me in its hold.

"Hi," he said.

My parents came to the porch as I went to Mike.

"I stole everything . . . I—I—I thought she'd love
me," I said. "If . . . if I just—I took the mealies and
the waxworms and the supers and the ham—I . . . I
thought I could make her love me," I said. "All the
toys—"

Caught my breath.

"I took the hamster ball," I said. "I—you were with the fish—the toys—my pack—the worms . . . I took it all—you were—I could have killed her," I said. "I almost—"

Mike's arm was around my shoulder . . . my parents, me, and him—we stood on the porch together.

"I must owe you. I took SO—"

Then I could hear my father, from that day so long ago, even as he stood right there.

Breathe.

Remember to breathe.

And I breathed in, as slowly as I could—and I let it out the same. . . .

"How can I make it up?" I said. "What can I do? There must be some—"

"Hey," Mike said. "You lost your friend . . . you lost your friend, and I didn't know what to do."

Mike kept me in his hold, not letting go.

They'd all wanted to help me when I couldn't be helped. I looked at my dad, my mom, Mike. . . . They'd seen the terrible, awful things I could do, and they were still by my side—

Breathe.

"The stuff," my dad said. "We'll cover it, of course..."

"Can I do *something?*" I said to Mike. He'd come to check on me, even after I ran. He was looking out for me, and I hardly knew him. This guy, this salesclerk from Total Pets. .... "Cleaning tanks? Crickets? Checking worms? Anything? Please?"

"I'm just happy you're all—"

"Please?"

"If you want to that badly," he said, "I could use some help."

"Not with the fish, though," I said. It just came out.

"*Everyone* starts with the fish," he said. "No exemptions." And I felt a little smile, creeping, creeping out, making its way onto my face.

Mike told us the tail would grow back as long as I kept the vivarium clean.

I didn't know about Matylda or Guy, though— didn't know if they could forgive me, too. So much to say and so little to say. I went upstairs and put my face to the glass. Matylda came over to me, her body so short now, and we were almost touching except for the glass, No-Tail Matylda of the Strawberry Stump.

"Not going to fight it anymore," I said.

She was listening.

"Your tail will grow back," I continued. "It won't look quite the same, but it'll be a tail." She had an expression on her face like she knew—we'd both lost and won at the same time, but with love, not like in Monopoly. As if she understood that I had to almost lose her to know how much I loved her. I loved her my way. From the beginning, there had been a wisdom about her. She, more than anyone, knew that love sometimes came with a price.

"I love you, Matylda," I said. And I breathed in and I let myself go, and my lizard girl met me there with her gaze, both of us softened to the world. "I can't do it his way," I said, "and it might not be enough to cover us both, but I'll give you all I have.

"I'll never be the same, either," I said. "You and me, Matylda with a *y*, we're different now. I can't love you with a wagonful of flowers, 'cause I'm not Guy. But I love you anyway."

And she bowed, the same way she had when I first found my words, under the towel that day so long ago, and I think she was telling me I'd get all she had, too. I bowed back to her then, my mind open to the world and the secrets it held.

Chapter Thirty-Two

Sky grey, weather still warm.

"Your tail's coming back," I said to Matylda. It wasn't too long since it had dropped, and I was keeping crickets out of the vivarium just in case they wanted to nibble. Mike said they might do that. Had to make sure her new tail grew strong. The pink tissue inside had grown first, with all her spots still there, the bumpy yellow skin covering after, the black spots on the outer skin lining up with the ones inside. She was healing, but you could tell something had happened. That was right—we wouldn't forget this, either of us. We each had a new identity, but only together with who we'd been before. We were all between two worlds, when I thought about it.

I'd cleaned up the vivarium the day I nearly killed her, after Mike left, swept up the worms, changed my own bed, too. Didn't want my mom to do it anymore.

Recycled the toys—couldn't use them again after that. Didn't want them—didn't need them.

But I saved the tail, keeping it safe, in my jewelry box.

"It's time to bury it," I said to her.

My parents were there in the yard when the Hoses arrived—Mike, too. I'd invited them all. I was glad they'd come to join us; we all belonged together. Mrs. Hose looked different, like she could be sad and happy at the same time. I put my hands on both sides of my hat; it fit perfectly, coming down below my ears and not too tight. I was wearing it for all of us, even Guy. Somehow, I knew he was sticking with me, even though I'd broken my promise. There was forgiveness in the air.

"I've got a spot picked out," I said. Mrs. Hose followed me, and I went down on my knees, smoothing the ground with my same hands, my own strong hands, Matylda of the Bright and Tender New Tail on my neck. There, in front of the honeysuckle, sweet-smelling vine, sweet-tasting vine, I dug a hole; the earth smelled good, rich and moist, deep. I didn't dig down too far, just far enough to make a memorial and keep it close. I placed the tail there, as a little sun poked its way through the clouds, a little golden spot in the greyness.

My head down, I closed my eyes, and there was Guy, at the top of Matylda's mountain—I was with him; she was on my shoulder. We were on bicycles, and the road widened before us and we cycled down, the spokes spinning within the wheels, beautiful silvery flashing, turning, carrying us as we pedaled, all three together, all one.

Guy took his hands off the handlebars and cupped them over his mouth. *I LOVE YOU, SUSSY,* he shouted, *FOREVER AND ALWAYS.* I knew it was Guy, and my heart felt like it might explode with joy; despite everything, he still loved me. Despite everything, he believed in me. Despite everything, he was still around.

CAWOOOOOOHAH! I yelled back to Guy, *I LOVE*

YOU TOO! my words carried by the wind, my hands firmly on the bars, my feelings sure. I felt Matylda's starfish toes holding tighter, I felt her trust, and I felt her love, right on my shoulder.

"I love you," I whispered, turning to her, my breath warm on her face as she snuggled up tighter on my shoulder.

"He's here," I told them all, turning outward. "For always. I know that now. Sometimes the world's an imperfect circle." I opened my arms. "It's still a circle, though." Adjusted my hat. "Good-bye and hello," I said, trampoline in the corner of my eye. I could see a day, not too far away, the lunch-table boys and me, with Guy in the middle of it all, jumping up to the sky, where all the birds were singing, no ceiling out in the yard.

I put some dirt over the tail. Stuck my cherry-pie spoon in, firm and upright, so we wouldn't forget where we buried it.

Stood up then, my warrior still close, back-stepped my way to Mrs. Hose. Her arms circling round, welcoming me.

Survivors all.

Me and my hat, Mike, the Hoses, my parents, Matylda.

And Guy.

Not alone, not good-bye . . .

Not here, but here anyway.

Acknowledgments

Thank you to Michael, Charlotte, McGhee, Marshall, and Foster—my family. You saw me in my sorrow and joy and tears and hope and you didn't run away—instead you came closer and helped me be brave. And especially you, Charlotte—the oldest, you've been with us the longest—you were a light— a beautiful voice saying Go On.

I couldn't have gone on, though, had I not had the company of some people with incredibly kind hearts—you kept me going with your words at different points as I tried to find my way: Sunyung Ahn, Jenny Brown, Kate DiCamillo, Caitlyn Dlouhy,

Meg Leder, Karla Greenleaf-MacEwan, Jandy Nelson, Kathy Nuzum, David Small, Christine Snell, and Jeanne Steig.

When I finally did have a draft, it was for you, Joanna Cotler—you were waiting, arms open, welcoming those pages. Then you gave me your attention, belief, spirit, love—and your extraordinary art, which is so full of life and freedom and beauty.

Kathi Appelt, I can never thank you enough for taking a turn in the director's chair, for the "Kathi treatment," for your love and generosity—you floored me time and time and time again. *Sister sister sister!*

And my kinfolk, who are my roommates and my colleagues and my dear friends—you were passionate readers, thinkers, supporters—in it for the long haul: My agent, Elena Giovinazzo—you waited and believed, and then read it again and again and believed, newborn Robby kitty notwithstanding. You are steady in the rockiest seas—a shining shiny star. Courtney Stevenson—so new to this game—and at the same time so sure and helpful. And Heather Alexander, your glorious, buoyant words came right on time.

Hilary Van Dusen, my editor: from the first, you loved this story as your own, and you never hesitated to give me your time and your insight—no matter was too small. I cherish your guidance and humor and logic—your scientific focus and your deep understanding—your wisdom and belief and dispatch.

Rachel Smith, interior designer—thank you for your attention and artistry (and your hand-drawn spots). Matt Roeser, thank you for this amazing jacket.

And to all the Pippins I work with as a literary agent—thank you for inspiring me, as you do the work and make the world bigger and brighter with your words and pictures.

Last, my joy, my gratitude, my infinite wonder—to Margaret Klenck. You heard it first and you heard it last and you heard it in the middle . . . you listened with fierceness. Thank you for holding my story safely these years . . . and so much more.

I believe in the magic of this world.